Praise for Liz Bankes'

Irresistible

'Compelling, juicy, and highly enjoyable.'
Chicklish

'A quick, fun read . . . I will be keeping my eye
out for more books by Bankes in the future.'
Once Upon a Bookcase

'Great, chemistry-filled scenes.'
Fluttering Butterflies

'A fun debut [with] some genuinely
laugh-out-loud moments.'
Daisy Chain Book Reviews

'Simply irresistible, truly one of those rare reads
that captivated me . . . amazing.'
Totally Bookalicious

'Really absorbing – should Mia stick with
good-guy Dan or follow her heart and dive
into a rocky relationship with Jamie?
A real page-turner!'
Amber, 16

'An enthralling insight into the inner workings
of teenage lif

From an early age Liz Bankes wanted to be a Thunderbird. Upon discovering that they were fictional and wooden she decided to be a writer. She wrote her GCSE coursework about a woman who cooks people in pies, and later won the Tunbridge Wells Girls Grammar School creative writing prize.

She went on to study book-reading at some universities in order to avoid getting a job and to spend the next four years in pyjamas. After working on a building magazine and a science magazine, she had the wonderful and very exciting chance to write a story.

As well as all book-related things, she also likes comedy and cats.

Unstoppable

LIZ BANKES

Piccadilly

First published in Great Britain in 2014
by Piccadilly Press
A Bonnier publishing company
Northburgh House, 10 Northburgh Street, London EC1V 0AT
www.piccadillypress.co.uk

A catalogue record for this book is available from the British Library.

ISBN: 978 1 84812 360 1 (paperback)
978 1 84812 361 8 (ebook)

1 3 5 7 9 10 8 6 4 2

Printed and bound by CPI Group (UK) Ltd, Croydon, CR0 4YY

To Mum and Dad
For making the home I always want to come back to
(and not complaining when I do).

Worries.

1. I will fall over/break all the computers/kill the office hamster on the first day of the work placement, get sacked and then have to come home.

2. All the people I'll meet in Oxford will think I'm weird and I won't have any friends.

3. Living in Cal's house will mean he discovers that I shave my legs, I don't wake up with all my make-up already on (I can't do the sneaking to the loo at five a.m. thing every day) and that really I'm quite mental. As a result he'll leave me.

4. My parents will find out that the 'spare room' I told them I'm living in at Cal's is actually a cupboard and I am really staying in his room. They will insist I come home and he will think I'm a child. As a result he'll leave me.

5. I worry that I worry too much.

1

They exchange looks, wondering whether or not to carry on the conversation. I forget sometimes they all grew up here, whereas I only moved here when I started at the college. Mia and Gabi have been best friends since they were tiny. Nish was part of a different crowd – the private school crowd who used to hang out in the pool house of the castle Jamie's parents own. Then Mia got a summer job at the castle. So they have all this gossip and history on people that I don't know, including Cleo.

'It's been two years. She might have got less hot,' says Gabi brightly, oblivious to the looks she's getting from the other two. 'And maybe less scary and evil.'

Scary and evil?

Mia sees my face.

'She had a reason to be scary and evil,' she says. 'I sort of, you know, stole her boyfriend. And Gabi's right – it was ages ago. Has anyone even seen her since that summer?'

Nish shakes her head. 'Her parents were always moving countries, so she changed schools again. Effie and I haven't heard much from her. Only rumours.'

'What rumours?' I say without thinking and Nish shakes her head.

'Oh, it was probably all bollocks.'

'You told me one of them was that she seduced a teacher,' says Gabi.

'Really?' says Nish.

'Yeah,' says Gabi. 'And you said that she broke up the marriage of one of her friend's parents.'

'You seem to have developed an excellent memory.' Nish

18

Cal to call me to

I haven't spok

yesterday morni

last night and th

Did I text him

My mum's

distracting my

and *unemploy*

whose key ski

things to wor

Maybe a s

Okay, pag

What if (

died?

His hous

while. They

Or, even

Even wc

if Cal was

Maybe,

Thankf

conclusior

hopeful, o

be about t

b) is alive

Unles

Woul

I bala

fish the

sits up on her elbows and fixes Gabi with a look.

'And she . . .' Gabi trails off as she sees Nish's expression. There is a moment of silence.

'Mia's got an STD!' Gabi exclaims.

'Er, what?' Mia stops rocking the chair and it hits the floor with a clunk.

'Okay, she doesn't actually. I was just changing the subject,' says Gabi. 'But if she did have one, what do we think it would be?'

'Herpes,' says Nish instantly.

Everyone bursts out laughing and Mia throws a cuddly toy that hits Nish square in the face. I get this sudden strong aching feeling to not go away for the summer. To stay with my friends and get a normal summer job and keep seeing Cal at weekends.

Seeing as at the end of the summer we'll all be going off to do completely different things. Nish is doing economics at Exeter. Mia's going to live in Australia for a year with Jamie. Gabi's not leaving – she didn't apply for uni and she's going to go full-time at Radleigh Castle, where she waitresses and helps organise events.

And I'm off to Manchester to do business studies.

My tactic is to not think about it too much, so I can pretend it's not looming and only two months away and I'm not terrified. I tune back into the conversation again. It's moved from STDs to Gabi and Max. About how when she visits him at uni they still share a bed and no one, except Gabi, thinks that's normal. She says that it just feels so nice they are best friends that she doesn't want to ruin it by

'Um . . . no

'You sure?'

'Yes, thank

I start pull

and put it or

knock into it

phone.

Once I'v

the bagel ar

before I sta

I need to r

"Scuse

'I don't

She ho

'Sorry,

The tr

a nice ga

pram nee

wall with

I thir

things a

to Mak

Knowi

I w

that if

Pag

is full

to the

in. I f

I mumble into the phone, 'I love you, you sexy pig.'

'Louder,' he says firmly. I know Cal and I know I'm fighting a losing battle.

'I love you, you sexy pig,' I say.

'I said, tickets, please.' In the space of about two seconds the woman's face has been replaced by the ticket inspector.

'Oh! Sorry.' I fumble in my bag. 'I was just on the phone to my boyfriend.' I hold up the phone to show him, but there's nothing there. I must have lost signal. The inspector goes and the woman's face is back again. She's giving me an odd look.

I turn away and pick up the folder again, trying to keep in mind what Cal always says. You'll never see these people again. What does it matter what they think?

Right. Page one.

Dear M,

There is an animal in the house. It brushed past my leg at dinner and when I asked what the fuck it was, Cal looked up and said, 'It's a cat.'

I quite reasonably asked if someone could get rid of it and Arlo looked horrified and told me that 'Nigel' lives here. I said 'Oh, does he?' and Cal said 'She' without even looking up from his food.

When I asked why none of them had thought to mention this before, Arlo laughed and said, 'She's part of the house – like the sofa or something. We didn't mention the sofa in the interview either.'

I told him that was slightly different as the sofa isn't going to give me fleas and it doesn't shit in a box. Then Dan said, 'She goes outside' and gave me a brief smile before carrying on eating.

So, Dan. When I knew him he was Mia's boyfriend and the kitchen boy at Radleigh Castle. Everyone always went on about him being 'lovely and funny', which means 'sweet but dull', and I didn't bother speaking to him.

And he is. Nice and funny. Friendly, but not loud. He makes tea for people in the morning. He likes puns, which is slightly tiresome, but better than no sense of humour, I suppose. I just feel like there's something else there – there's an edge to things he says sometimes and it's got me interested. I might try and seduce him, just for fun. Haven't done that in a while.

The rest of them are falling over themselves to do my

27

laundry/take me to Asda/get me to join in with 'board game night'. Arlo came to my room on my second evening here to 'get to know me better'. He was here for a whole fucking hour. It's exhausting talking to people without actually telling them anything.

So, the cat. Just now, when I started writing this, I heard this scraping sound. I looked over at the window and there was the cat, doing this weird frantic scratching thing on the glass. So I walked over and shut the curtain. Seriously, what is it with pets? I had to put up with Mum buying kittens all over the place when I was little. And then obviously we'd move house so she had to give them away. She clearly gave that as much thought as she gives anything. One time they bought me a kitten, to try and make me less antisocial. (I think this was around the time I would get sent home from school for biting.) The thing kept following me around and would not take the hint. So I decided to freak my parents out by becoming really attached to it and insisted on taking it everywhere we went. They finally took it away when I told them I wanted to cut off its paws so it couldn't run away from me.

Are you with me on this? Or did you secretly have some beloved childhood dog that you let lick your face? God, I hope not.

I got the feeling when I met you that you were with me on most things. You strode into the quad like you belonged there. Not like everyone else – nervously gulping too much champagne and comparing A-Level results to see if they were the cleverest here like they were at school. You looked *like you were doing everyone a favour just by turning up. You didn't even have your gown on properly. And those green Converse – the Master's wife nearly had a stroke.*

I opened the window to have a cigarette in the end, so the sodding cat came in. It walked over and sat on this letter, so I had to move it to keep on writing and it sat on my lap. I gave up and let it stay. Then I read it the letter. So I've started talking to cats. Tragic, really. But then I tried having a real friend once and look how that turned out.

I'd better go now. My attendance is required at another party. I've gone from champagne in the old library to beer from a bucket. I just heard Simon walk past my room and say, 'Do you think she'd want to play strip poker?'

I'll leave you with that image.

Love you.

Cleo x

Chapter 4

I see him as the train is pulling into the station. As usual he's managed to persuade them to let him through the barriers to come and wait for me on the platform. As usual he's towering over everyone else. 'Big' is a word you associate with Cal. He's six foot three and chunky. He has a big grin. And a big heart.

Once when we were playing Articulate, Mia was trying to act out 'whale' and she said 'big' and without thinking I said 'Cal'. They have never let me forget it.

He spots me as I step off the train and comes jogging over. Before I have the chance to get out of the way of the people behind me, he's put his arm round me, pulled me into his chest and given me a big kiss on the side of the face.

'Can you move?' says a drawling voice. 'People need to get past . . .'

'Oh, sorry!' says Cal and we step to the side to let the guy who sat in my seat get off the train. 'Come on through, pal!'

The way Cal talks, like it hadn't even occurred to him that we might be in the way, completely disarms the guy and he splutters thanks at us as he goes.

'Right,' says Cal, picking up my bag and offering me his arm. 'We still have time to go to the bench before it closes. Let's go!'

It takes ten minutes of sitting on our bench to make me realise I've been an idiot the last few days. We are completely enclosed by the warmth of the garden. It's in the mottled green shadows cast by the trees, in the mixture of fresh and sharp scents and in the bench itself, heated up by the sun. But most of all it's the feeling I get from leaning my head on Cal's shoulder as he tells me all about the curry club challenge. I can feel the muscles in his neck moving as he speaks and his arm tensing when he gets to exciting bits in the story (which is often).

There are occasional shrieks from the river behind us as people hiring punts discover that punting isn't as easy as it looks.

We did it during the heatwave in the spring, with me, Cal and Dan on one boat and Arlo, Simon and one of their old housemates, Millad, on the other. I managed to balance and get the boat going straight and quite smoothly, which I thought was impressive, even if the others took the piss out of us for how slow we were going. When Cal took control he tried to wave the pole over his head in a sort of

31

war dance, lost control of it and knocked Dan in.

We can't stay long because the garden closes at six and because other people walk past, wanting to look at the bench. That's because it's not really our bench, it's Will and Lyra's bench. But we come here, even if it's only for ten minutes, every time I visit. It was top of my list the first time I came to Oxford and it was how we found out that we both have the same favourite book. We read the *His Dark Materials* books to each other sometimes. As we stand up to go, I look behind me at where someone has carved *Will* and *Lyra* inside a heart into the wood. Cal has a picture of it as his cover photo on Facebook. It feels like a secret message to me.

We walk over Magdalene Bridge and towards Cowley Road, where the house is. When we stop at the Sainsbury's on the roundabout to stock up for the house party I take my bag back and trail behind Cal as he picks up a crate of beer. I reply to Nish's text asking me how it's going with a smiley face.

It's a familiar sound. Cal's loud laugh as he stands at the centre of a group of people. It's the rugby team, who all meet up – even in the summer – for training and socials. Mostly socials, I think. It seems a million times louder when they're all together and the living room is taken over by the noise. Cal is always in the middle. Not because he's the most extroverted, or tells the craziest stories, but just because he's so comfortable, I think. He's so relaxed and happy with who he is and that's something people warm to. He's also wearing the lederhosen that Dan got him from Germany.

Cal must be talking about me because for a moment the whole group looks over at me. People must wonder why someone so fun is going out with someone so quiet. Sometimes they think I'm fun by association and I worry that at some point they'll discover that I'm a fraud. I try, but it's not easy when you run everything you want to say round and round your head first to check that it isn't weird. Then when you finally pluck up the courage to say it, the moment's passed and they've moved on to talking about something else.

I'll have another gulp of wine.

I think I'll try to sidle up to a conversation and try to join in without anyone noticing. This group look like they might be friendly. They seem to be talking about some sort of book or film or TV show that I don't catch the name of. But I start nodding along. The guy nearest to me notices and turns his head towards me.

'Are you a fan?'

I should just ask what it is. But I'm already nodding. I can't go back. 'Yeah,' I say, nodding even more vigorously. 'I love that . . .'

What is it? Book? Film? I have no idea.

'I love *that*.'

That's right – repeating it makes you sound like you know what you're talking about.

'What's your favourite bit?' he says.

'Oh, I just love the characters. They're great, aren't they?'

A few of them smile politely for a second and then go

back to their conversation, while I look around the room for a corner I can curl up and die in.

I spy Simon and Arlo standing in the kitchen. They'll talk to me. But when I get in there they are huddled into some sort of intense discussion and Simon is waving a pack of cards.

'I don't think she'll go for the strip poker. It's too obvious,' Arlo is saying.

'Hmm, planning something more subtle, are we?' Simon whispers, raising his eyebrows.

'Charm,' says Arlo, nodding.

Oh dear. Arlo is lovely, but I've only really heard him talk about computer games.

'I was definitely getting somewhere the other night. We had a heart-to-heart for *ages* and you know, she kept *showing me things*.' Arlo nods again, significantly.

'Like what?' says Simon.

I'm in that awkward position where you've walked into a room and no one's noticed. What's the best thing to say in that situation, which announces you are there and won't make people think you've been lurking?

'Like her legs,' says Arlo.

'She did not show you her legs!' says Simon scornfully.

Perhaps if I put this cup down loudly they'll see I'm here. No. They don't.

'She did!' says Arlo. 'Well, it's like, her legs were there and it was definitely for me to see.'

Simon scoffs. 'After tonight, she'll be showing me more than her legs.'

Now it's Arlo's turn to look sceptical.

'Yeah,' carries on Simon. 'She'll be showing me her . . .' There's a pause and a shuffle. '. . . vagina.'

'I'm here!' I say in a sing-song voice.

They start and look at me with slightly shocked expressions. I should have just gone with 'hello'.

'All right, Rosie?' says Arlo. Simon nods at me.

'Oh, good thanks. How are y—'

But they are already on their way out of the room and have gone back to their argument. I see some empty cocktail jugs on the side and think I may as well make myself useful. I hear the buzz of voices out in the hall and feel the quietness of the kitchen even more. I tell myself I'll just walk up to someone and introduce myself when I go back in. If I go back in with drinks that will be a talking point, anyway.

I take a breath and swallow the sad bubble that's crept into my throat. Then I feel warm arms slide round my waist. Cal rests his chin on top of my head.

'Good evening,' he says. He has his hands either side of me on the kitchen worktop. I turn round and wrap my arms around his neck. Our lips meet and he moves against me. Everything else melts away. Then he looks at me with the face I love – like he's trying not to smile too much.

I slide my hands on to his shoulders and flick the strap of the lederhosen.

'Ah.' Cal nods and he puts on a ridiculous German accent. 'Zis you find sexy?'

'Very,' I say and ping the strap again.

'Ow!' he laughs and leans in to kiss me.

'Guys, guys!' Simon and Arlo come crashing back through the door.

'We're going to play spin the bottle!' says Arlo breathlessly.

'Awesome,' says Cal as they run back out again. He plays with a strand of my hair. 'I guess we should rejoin the party.' He wrinkles his nose.

'Yeah, wouldn't want to miss the gossip!' I say and start towards the door. But Cal still has hold of my hand and I stop.

'I'd rather stay in here and have a kiss,' he says.

This is how it goes every time. He feels like he has to rescue me. To come and hide in an empty room just because I am.

'They'll think I'm keeping you from the fun. Come on!' My voice is way more bright than normal. I sound mental.

I tug at his arm.

'Ugh!' he says and follows me, grabbing his beer from the side as we leave.

Chapter 5

Cleo is standing outside the living-room door, blowing smoke out of her mouth. She has a cigarette, obviously, although for a moment I have an image of her as some supernatural dragon woman.

She looks effortlessly elegant in a short black dress with lace at the bottom. But the impact is not quite the same as a few hours ago when she walked into Cal's room wearing just her underwear to let us know the bathroom was free.

I'd just arrived so had my hair scraped up on top of my head and I was nice and sweaty after walking from the station. Her hair was like in the pictures I looked at – in ringlets cascading around her shoulders.

Cleo stopped when she saw me and frowned. 'Who are you?'

'This is Rosie,' said Cal. 'She's staying for the summer.

I've been talking about it all week!'

'Oh right,' said Cleo. 'Sorry – I find stuff like that really boring. Why are you doing that, then?'

'Um, I don't know really,' I said, caught off guard and temporarily misplacing my brain.

'She has a super-amazing work placement,' said Cal.

'Lovely,' said Cleo. And then walked out.

I thought about saying something about the fact that she'd not been wearing any clothes, but I didn't. Nish says I need to 'keep the crazy in'. Gabi thinks I should let it out and hope he loves me anyway.

Dan comes down the stairs and tells Cleo to take it outside, gesturing at the cigarette. He says it in a good-natured way, though.

'Sorry, Dad,' she says and rolls her eyes at Cal.

'Oh, he dances like a dad too, don't you, dude?' says Cal.

Dan turns round. 'My dancing is for your eyes only, babe.' He blows Cal a kiss, then sees me hovering behind. 'Oh hey, Rosie!'

I smile and say, 'Hello', except my voice catches in my throat and it comes out like a croaky growl.

Dan's too polite to reference it, so he just says, 'All right?' and I nod and smile because I don't want to risk growling again. Dan is someone I can turn to in these situations – he's lovely and doesn't judge me for being socially inept. He'll just make a joke or something so I can relax.

I wonder if he and Cleo ever met when he was working at Radleigh?

* * *

'What's this game then?' says Cleo, in a bored tone.

'Spin the bottle,' says Cal. 'Are you playing?'

Did he say it hopefully?

Stop it, Rosie. Keep the crazy in.

Cleo shrugs. 'Sure, why not? I'm a good kisser.'

We follow her into the room. I don't know if Cal and I are supposed to be playing or if we're just watching. What are the rules for something like this? We're probably supposed to be so secure in our love for one another that we can sit around casually kissing other people and not be bothered by it.

Cleo sits on the arm of the sofa next to where Cal's just sat down on the floor.

I would definitely be bothered by it.

Gradually everyone arranges themselves into a circle. I think for one (not very logical) moment that we'll have to introduce ourselves like on the first day of college where we all had to say an interesting fact about ourselves.

I go to sit near Cal, but he pulls me over so I'm sitting in-between his legs. Then he puts his hands on my waist and traces circles on my hips. I lean back against his chest.

Simon gets things started by putting a bottle in the middle of the circle. 'Just so you know, ladies, this is my bottle. So think about that when you have your hands around it,' he says.

No one says anything, although a few people groan in disgust, so he carries on.

'If anyone wants to spin my bottle in real life, my room's just up there.' He winks.

'That doesn't even make sense,' says Arlo.

Someone else shouts for him to hurry up.

The first spin is a blond girl I don't know. And when she spins she gets Dan, who gives her a half smile and crawls forward. She rolls her eyes, but looks excited.

'That's Liv,' Cal whispers to me. 'Dan has a major crush on her.'

Just before he gets to her Dan stops and says, 'Wait.'

'What are you doing?' shouts Cal. 'Kiss her, dude!'

'I'm trying to make sure I don't bottle it . . .' says Dan and a groan goes up around the room. The girl shakes her head, but can't fight away a smile.

Their kiss goes on so long it has to be broken up by an impatient Simon, who is constantly edging closer to Cleo on the sofa, who in turn is leaning away from him, so much so that her hand is hanging over the arm of the sofa. Just by Cal's leg.

Dan spins and it takes ages to stop. It comes to a halt pointing towards our side of the room.

'Cleo!' says Cal.

Across the circle, Arlo and Liv – who Dan just kissed – have very similar expressions of wide-eyed jealousy that they are trying to turn into smiles. Cleo's hand moves away from Cal's leg as she starts to get up.

'It was Simon,' Dan says.

Cleo stops.

'What?' says Simon.

'It's clearly Cleo,' says Cal and there are murmurs of agreement from around the room. Arlo is now looking at Dan like he's insane.

'If there's something else you'd rather be doing don't let

me stop you,' says Cleo. 'I can find you some pots to wash if you want.'

Dan shrugs. 'No, we may as well get it over and done with.'

Cleo blinks in surprise and then sinks back into the sofa. 'Fine. Well, come and get it.'

'Bet that's not the first time you've said that.' Dan grins as he gets up.

People laugh, but it's in a kind of stilted way. That's not Dan's usual style of joke.

He leans over and their lips meet for about a second before he pulls back. They look at each other and for a moment I think they are going to lean back in again. But they don't and Dan returns to his place on the other side of the circle.

Cleo gets up to do her spin. Lots of the guys shift around and look like they might be trying to take up more room in the circle.

I wish I could just be a nice person and that my heart didn't sink every time there is a clear sign of how much everyone fancies her. Or that I didn't secretly wish that Cal had only male friends. That's the worst bit – I don't even have the right to feel like this.

'Cal!'

Oh no.

'Hey, we're just watching,' Cal says and howls of protest go up around the room. My chest feels empty.

Cleo raises an eyebrow at Cal and he tilts his head towards her and holds his thumb out questioningly. It takes me a moment to work out what he's suggesting. Cal stands up and leans over towards the sofa. They link hands and then move their heads together. The idea is that it looks like they're kissing, but actually all they are doing is kissing their own thumbs. Cal exaggerates it to make it look ridiculous and Cleo plays along too.

But it still looks like they are kissing.

Cal takes a bow and sits down and then Cleo says, 'So is no one going to kiss me properly, then?'

There's a silence, before one of the rugby guys shouts, 'Rosie should do it on his behalf!' Another one joins in. 'Yeah, it's not cheating if you kiss another girl.'

Cleo turns to look at him for a second and blinks. There's a glint in her eyes that suggests she could rip him apart if she wanted to. He goes red and shrinks back towards the wall. Then she turns to me.

'Oh come on,' she says and grabs my face, pulling me upwards.

Our lips meet and press together. An unexpected rush fills my chest. A couple of people cheer and whistle around the room. And then we pull apart, like she did with Dan, but her hands are still on my cheeks and she stops me moving back. I just have time to notice that her eyes are closed before she moves in again. This time our lips are only just touching and I hear her intake of breath, like she is savouring it. Her fingers grip my cheeks tighter and she presses her mouth against mine again.

Well, she wasn't lying about being a good kisser.

As I sit back down Cleo seems to be looking past me.

I turn to Cal, who is staring at me in astonishment.

Cal spins and gets Simon, who lets out a cry of protest. Cal launches himself across the room, calls out, 'Come here, you sexy beast,' and plants a kiss right on his lips.

The room is full of whoops and laughter, but when I look at Cleo, she's staring into space. Suddenly she stands up and takes the attention of the whole room with her.

'I'm going out,' she says vaguely and walks out of the door.

Dear M,
So many things reminded me of you tonight.
Cleo x

Chapter 6

I go into the bathroom to clean my teeth and find two girls in there, one sitting on the toilet and one on the edge of the bath. I realise one of them is Liv, who kissed Dan earlier. When I ask if I can come in and clean my teeth she nods at me briefly and turns back to the conversation.

'Yeah, I know, he is so lovely. He's, like, really sweet, you know?'

'Do you think you'll ask him out?' says her friend.

'Maybe,' Liv considers. 'I mean, Dan is lovely. But then there's Kurt.'

'But he's a complete dick to you,' her friend retorts.

'Yeah, I know.'

'You didn't hear from him for two weeks and then he sent you a picture of his penis that was meant for someone else.'

'Yeah, I know.'

'And he told you that you could go out with him as long as he didn't have to acknowledge you as his girlfriend to anyone.'

'Yeah, I know. He's a total dick. But it's kind of hot, do you know what I mean?'

I watch them in the mirror. This Liv seems like a bit of an idiot to me. Her friend needs to put her straight.

'Yeah, he's hot,' the girl agrees.

'Come on!' I say, forgetting that I am not actually in the conversation. And that I have a mouthful of toothpaste, some of which bubbles out of my mouth. I try to suck it back in and see the girls looking over at me and in a panic I swallow.

For a moment we are just looking at each other, while my throat burns.

'Did you just swallow your toothpaste?' says the second girl.

'Yeah,' I say in a husky, wheezing voice and making my throat sting even more. 'Are you not meant to?'

'No!' They both stare at me like I am an utter freak.

'Ah, well. Good to know for next time. Thanks, pals!'

Pals? I need to go and live in a cave.

'Weird . . .' I hear Liv mutter as I leave. I find it slightly depressing to be called weird by someone who thinks being sent accidental penis pictures is hot.

Dan is standing in the corridor outside the bathroom, leaning against the wall and frowning. I wonder how long he's been there?

'Oh, hey!' he says, his face brightening. 'I think it's the time of night for *Guitar Hero*.' He holds up the box.

He seems to be hovering here in the hall. Maybe he's waiting around for the chance to talk to Liv.

'How are you, Dan?' My voice has almost returned to normal now.

'Oh,' he says, 'I'm not so bad. Mustn't fret . . .' He holds up the guitar and I laugh. 'I can't tempt you with a game?'

'Oh no – I've got my induction on the work placement thing tomorrow. Don't want to stagger in there with red eyes and fall off the chair and . . .'

Just stop talking.

'. . . wet myself.'

This is why I need to run things through my head before I say them. When I try to ad-lib, this happens.

'No, that wouldn't get you a job,' says Dan. 'Unless perhaps they were interviewing for the town drunk.'

Dan is one of those people who goes with whatever stupid thing you've said, rather than pointing out how stupid it is.

'I hope it goes well, anyway,' he says and starts down the stairs. 'I think Cal will be up soon – he said he had something in the morning, too.'

Chapter 7

'What do you need to get up for?' I ask Cal as he shuts his bedroom door.

'Huh?' he says. 'Hey, check this out!'

He starts humming some made-up cabaret tune. Then he lunges forward, throws his head back and pouts at me. He pulls one of the braces of his shorts off his shoulder and arches his eyebrow coyly.

'Hmm ... I'm guessing you're supposed to be some sort of stripper?' I laugh.

'Oh yeah,' says Cal breathily. He pings the other strap and then rolls it down. Then he puts his hands behind his head and thrusts his hips in a circle.

'It's terrifying,' I tell him.

'Me being sexy is terrifying?' he says, pretending to be hurt.

'It's monstrous!' I say.

He laughs and then turns round in front of me and does the hip-thrusting thing again, only this time his bum is right in my face. He wiggles it from side to side. Me laughing spurs him on. He hums even louder and the moves get even more flamboyant. Soon I can't breathe. I reach forward and yank the lederhosen down.

Cal spins round with a look of mock outrage.

'Right.'

He climbs out of the shorts, leaps on to the bed and pins me down. The laughter subsides and then at the same moment we both break into a smile. I slide my hands out from under his, wrap them round his neck and pull him down onto me and we kiss. Then there's the hurried untangling of legs as we take off our clothes. We've worked out by now that there is no elegant way of doing it. Especially not with knickers. It's more about speed. Obviously Cal is ready first as he's hardly wearing anything. He lies on his side, watching me, and then laughs when my dress gets stuck on my head.

We kiss for ages, running fingers along each other's bodies and delaying the moment for as long as we can stand it. When he finally pushes inside me we both sigh with relief.

'I've been waiting for that,' he whispers, as he kisses my neck and I dig my fingers into his shoulder.

We lie there, my head on his chest, as our breathing slowly returns to normal.

Every so often a particularly loud shout or laugh carries up the stairs as the party continues.

'I wonder where Cleo went,' says Cal suddenly.

'Yeah, I don't know,' I reply.

Keep the crazy in.

'I know it's early days, but she hasn't hung around with us much,' he says.

'No?'

'She stays in her room all the time. I think she might be quite shy.'

I laugh into his chest.

'What?' He twists his head so he can see me.

'I don't think shy people walk around in their underwear.'

Careful.

The silence that follows seems to last hours.

'I walk round in my underwear and I'm terribly shy.' Cal looks at me with serious eyes. I poke him in the stomach and he laughs.

'It's true. I am ever so shy.'

I look up at his profile, the corner of his mouth in a slight smile. It's one of those moments when I want to squeeze him and not let go.

'Don't you want to go down and keep walking around in your underwear?' I say.

'I'd rather stay here with you,' he says. 'For ever.' He kisses the top of my head. 'Till you're old and dead.'

'Even if I have no teeth and a hump?'

'Especially if you have no teeth and a hump.'

'Even if I smell of wee and go round town with a

shopping trolley full of cats, shouting at children?'

'Rosie, don't pretend that's got anything to do with being old – you did that the other day.'

I press myself closer against him. It's funny how in some ways Cal is the person I'm least self-conscious around with what I say, but at the same time I haven't told him half the things that are going through my head.

Chapter 8

I wake up a few hours later and reach out for him, but just find my hand sliding onto the empty sheet. He must have gone out to go to the loo.

I really need it too, come to think of it. And there's only one in the house. That's something that will take some getting used to over the summer. I wait a few minutes, staring out at the room, which is blue in the moonlight. My suitcase is still lying against the wardrobe. As I only arrived two hours before the party started I didn't have a chance to unpack. Although to be honest I'm not totally sure where my stuff is going to go. Cal is not the tidiest person in the world and keeps his stuff in piles on the floor. He promised he would sort out the room and make some space for my things before I arrived, but it never happened.

Dad texted me last night and said we should Skype so he

can see my room. I ignored that bit of the text, because if we did that then it would be quite obvious I am living in Cal's room.

Cal hasn't come back. I could go and knock to get him to hurry up. I slide out from under the duvet and after a few minutes' searching manage to locate my pyjamas on the floor. I creep down to the bathroom quickly, as I am actually becoming desperate now.

It's empty.

Coming back up the stairs a few minutes later I see something that I managed to completely miss in my urgent dash. Even though the landing has only reached a dull summer glow there is clearly a crack of light coming out from under the door opposite Cal's. Cleo's room.

And voices. Well, her voice.

And the creaks of feet moving around.

I didn't see any other lights on in other rooms when I went to the loo.

I edge closer to the door. But suddenly my breathing sounds creepy and loud, like a murderer in a film. And every step I take seems to creak a different floorboard. I panic and run back into Cal's room.

I stand there in the middle of the floor, completely still in the gloom, straining to hear above the sound of my heart thumping in my ears.

Twenty minutes later I'm still in exactly the same position and I think I have cramp. And Cal's still not back.

He might have got up to have a midnight feast.

In the dark.

Or maybe he's dead again?

Again. Because he was dead all the other times, wasn't he, you insane woman.

I walk back over towards the bed, but get distracted by a sudden hum from the computer. It's on.

Maybe there'll be a clue on there about where he is.

You know that you're being a psycho when you start finding reasonable justifications for stalking.

I move the mouse. The password screen comes up. I could try putting in 'rosie'. You know, just to see.

I'm in.

His desktop background is a picture of all the housemates from last year, having a picnic in the meadows. Cal is playing some bongos and wearing a giant false moustache.

I get a pang of guilt for snooping on him. But I get the pang as I am opening the browser and clicking on *History*, so it is an empty thought, really.

My eyes pass over all the Facebook pages, Law Soc emails, resit timetables, Netflix, and stop on one thing.

Spankathon.

Which he was watching yesterday, when I was on the train. Just before he called me.

Should I click on it?

I hover the mouse over the link. And click. Another browser window opens and starts loading. But then more windows and adverts start popping up and the screen is full of genitals.

Apparently there are 'loads of horny sluts' in my area now. So that's good to know.

And the speakers seem to be set at full volume, as suddenly

the room is full of moaning.

I fly into a panic and start frantically shutting down all the windows, but more keep popping up. It's like one of those games where you have to whack the moles with a mallet, except with spanking lesbians.

Then I hear footsteps outside the room.

I throw myself to the floor and pull the computer plug out of its socket.

The door opens and Cal walks in. He's wearing his boxers and a hoodie. He turns the door handle carefully so it doesn't make a sound and shuts the door. Then he looks over at the bed. And tries to peer more closely in the dark.

'Rosie?' he whispers.

'I'm on the floor,' I whisper back.

'Oh,' he says. It doesn't seem to occur to him to ask why, which is good. Because I can't think of anything to tell him that would sound sane.

'I couldn't sleep,' he says. 'Went for a walk around the block.'

In training for a spankathon?

'Weren't you cold in your boxers?' I say, getting back into bed and lying on my side, facing the wall.

He slides in behind me, puts his hand on my waist and kisses my cheek.

'Nah,' he says. Then he turns over, facing away from me as well. We have this unspoken rule where for sleeping we each have our own space.

'Love you,' he says.

'Love you, too.'

Chapter 9

Arlo and Simon are whispering to each other by the fridge when Cleo walks into the kitchen in a strappy top and tiny shorts.

'So who was he?' says Simon. He puts his hands on the back of one of the kitchen chairs and moves it back and forward in what is meant to be a casual manner. But he overdoes it by swinging his leg as well.

Cleo walks past and ignores him. 'Oh, a coffee would be lovely, Kitchen Dan,' she says, seeing him about to put the kettle on.

'Sure,' he says and flicks the switch on.

Cal is at the cooker poaching eggs, wearing only his woman's body apron and some pants.

'Who was who?' says Dan as he gets the mugs out.

'The person in Cleo's room last night,' says Simon with

another swing of the leg.

Cleo is sitting on one of the kitchen chairs with her knees drawn up to her chin. 'A management consultant,' she says.

'Without any shoes?' says Arlo suspiciously.

'What?' says Cleo.

'That's the sign when you bring someone home.' He nods, like he's imparting age-old wisdom. 'Shoes outside the door. There were no shoes outside Cleo's door and no extra shoes in the hall. I counted.'

'You need a life,' says Dan, moving Arlo out of the way to get to the fridge.

'Any girl who spends the night in my room won't ever need shoes, or clothes, again,' says Simon.

'That just sounds like you're going to kill them,' says Dan.

Arlo paces the room like he's a detective. 'So that means that it was someone who was at the party already.'

'Who wants my eggs?' Cal cuts in. Dan and I raise our hands. Simon and Arlo seem happy with Pop-Tarts. Cleo is probably one of those people who has a bowl of seeds for a meal and likes it.

'Super,' says Cal. 'Rosie, could you grab the toast?'

'Yep!' I say and smile. I tell myself I've been keeping the crazy in. I didn't ask him about the porn. Or if he was lying about the midnight walk. But I think really I'm waiting to see if he confesses or accidentally lets something slip.

Cleo takes a sip of the coffee that Dan has just put in front of her and then sees that Simon and Arlo are standing there staring at her. She sighs.

'What if his shoes were inside my room?'

Arlo's face falls. 'Oh yeah,' he says.

'A management consultant, out spending too much money in an overpriced club.' Cleo speaks in a tired, monotone way, like she's reading a shopping list. 'Thrilled to find someone up for doing the kinky stuff his boring wife won't do or has never heard of.'

Simon's eyes go wide and a bit of Pop-Tart falls out of Arlo's mouth.

Cal laughs as he puts the plates of eggs down on the table. 'That's mad!' he says.

About a million thoughts are zooming around my brain. So it wasn't Cal in her room? Unless she's lying. If she's not lying, is Cal interested? He looks interested. Is it the kinky stuff? We just do normal sex. Am I his boring wife?

'Married, eh?' says Dan. 'Nice.'

Cleo shrugs. 'I made a hundred quid out of it.'

'You do it for money?' says Arlo.

'Cool.' Simon nods.

'I was joking,' says Cleo.

'Oh, I knew that,' Arlo says. I think he'd been mentally working out how much money he has.

Chapter 10

'This seems to all be in order,' Gregory says as he looks through my form.

Does Cal want me to be more sexual? I can't even *say* things during sex. The one time I tried I said, 'Ooh, I like *that*,' and I reminded myself of a camp man and Cal looked at me oddly so I've never done it again.

'Is there anything you won't do?'

Bondage? Wearing one of those weird masks?

'Sorry?' I say, trying to focus.

'Well.' Gregory smiles. He's bald and in his thirties I think, with a pink, friendly face. 'It's just that some of the interns don't fancy call-centre stuff or companies with questionable ethics and that,' says Gregory.

'Oh, no, anything is fine. I ticked "okay" for everything in that sexual.'

'Um . . .' He pauses for a moment and his face turns a shade pinker. 'Cool, I . . .'

'I ticked everything in that *section*! On the form,' I say quickly.

I need to get a grip.

'Cool,' he says again. 'Awesome. Okay.' He gives me another smile and then clicks a few times on his mouse. A sheet of paper shoots out of the printer next to me. 'So we're allocating you this, starting Monday. If you'd like to cast your eyes over.'

WANT Lifestyle Solutions...

Job type: Customer Satisfaction Enabling Communications Operative.

'*WANT is a totally unique lifestyle management solutions provider that provides clients with the solutions before they even know they want them and addresses the needs they didn't know they had,*' Gregory reads off the screen. 'Want to give it a go?'

'Sure.' I nod. I don't really know what any of that means. And I am not sure you can call something 'totally unique'.

'Awesome,' says Gregory.

As he starts typing things from my form into his computer, I try to think of something other than Cal and Cleo and kinky sex.

'Right, I've entered you.'

Not helping, Gregory.

He clicks on something and then presses *Enter* with a flourish. 'All done!' he says and looks at the printer. Nothing happens. He turns back to the screen, clicks and presses *Enter* again. He keeps doing it, getting more and more

60

forceful, until he is slamming his hand down on the keyboard. Still nothing happens. He stops and stares at the screen.

'I hate my job,' he says.

'Oh . . . Oh dear,' I say.

He breathes out loudly, rests his forehead on his fist and scrunches up his face.

Should I say something? Or go over and hug him? Or just go?

He breathes out loudly again.

'Um . . .' I say.

The printer whirs into action and spits out another piece of paper.

'There we go!' He straightens up, grinning again. I take the piece of paper and put it in my bag.

'Good luck for Monday,' Gregory says, shaking my hand and nodding vigorously.

I start walking up the hill back out of town and decide to call my sister.

Poppy isn't exactly the sensible older-sister type. She's spent most of the last few years running off to different countries or getting involved in mad money-making schemes and then running out of money and calling up Mum and Dad to bail her out. But she's had a lot of boyfriends.

'ROSE!'

'Hey, how are you?'

'Yeah,' she says vaguely. 'Great. I'm in this big house with

61

all these people. We're like looking after it for some guy or something?'

'A squat?'

'Yeah, that's the one! So how's things, sis? You liking …' Poppy has trouble remembering what happened yesterday, let alone anything about my life. '… Scotland?'

'Oxford is great!' I say brightly. As if to emphasise the point, at that moment I come out of a passageway into the courtyard that has the pillared dome of one of the library buildings rising up at the centre of it. Its stone walls glow an orangey gold in the evening sun and as I stand in its shadow, surrounded by ancient college buildings, I forget for a moment that I am on the phone.

'Rose?'

'Sorry! Yes, I was, um, just wondering if I could get your advice about boys?'

'Totally. Ask me anything. I just broke up with this guy, actually. Shame – he was cool. Worked in sales.'

'Selling what?' I ask.

'Drugs mostly.'

'Oh, right.'

'And like these little wooden pigs?'

'Right. Normal,' I say. I realise I am only a road away from the pub Cal works in. I could go in and say hi to him before going back to the house.

'So why did you break up?' I ask Poppy as I go under an archway into another cobbled courtyard.

'I think he went to Asia to discover himself,' she says airily. 'Or Birmingham. What advice do you need? Have you had an argument with Steven?'

'Cal.'

'Really? Was he called Steven before?'

'No, he was never called Steven.'

'Weird.'

'Have you ever been worried that a guy was looking around for something else? That you weren't enough?'

She thinks for a moment.

'No.'

'Oh.'

'Look, Ro-bum, any guy that is looking around for something else when he's with you is a moron.'

'Maybe.'

'Not maybe – definitely. So stop worrying.'

'Okay,' I say. I don't think Poppy's ever worried in her life. When she was at primary school a group of girls started making fun of her because she's always been a bit overweight, and she just laughed.

And when this girl called Bea was bullying me in Year Seven, Poppy sat on her at the bus stop.

'And if he is cheating on you then punch him in the penis.'

'Right. Will do.'

The pub is hidden away off a side street and I make my way down the little alleyway that leads to it.

'Hey, sis?' says Poppy.

'Yeah?' I put my head in the door. He's not this side of the bar.

'I love you,' she says.

Or the other side. Maybe he's on the outside bar tonight.

'What do you want?' I say.

'Can I borrow some money?'

Gabi has joined the conversation.

Rosie: So what do you guys think? I'm going mad! Was in my Bright Sparx interview and the induction man, Gregory, was telling me all the details about the scheme and I didn't listen to anything he said. All I could think about was whether he wants me to be more sexual.

Mia: I don't think you need to worry.

Gabi: Why would the induction man want you to be sexual??

Mia: He might like watching that spanking lesbian stuff as a fantasy, but that doesn't mean he wants you to do it.

Gabi: What job are you doing??

Nish: Yeah, with you all he wants is to do what you're comfortable with. You don't have to go out and buy a load of whips and chains. I mean, unless you want to, obvs.

Gabi: I'm so confused.

Mia: Rosie found an 'interesting' video in Cal's internet history.

Gabi: Oh! That happened to me once.

Rosie: Really?

Gabi: Yeah. Max was upset because he thought it meant that I wanted him to be like that in real life. I told him that if he was like a male porn star in real life then

I wouldn't be able to stop laughing.

Mia: I don't think any of us would.

Gabi: Do you remember when we made our own?

Mia: Just to be clear – she means her and Max. Not her and me. And yes, I remember – you sent it to me!!

Gabi: Accidental!

Mia: It arrived when I was having tea with my parents. My stepdad glimpsed it over my shoulder and choked on a Jammy Dodger.

Nish: Guys – gross and hilaire, but focus. We are helping Rosie. Are you feeling reassured, Rosie?

Rosie: I am ☺

Nish: Hmm. What else is it?

Rosie: Nothing!

Nish: What else?

Rosie: It's just that with Cleo in the house I feel like even more of a boring loser. I think he'll look at her and see all the things I'm not.

Nish: Don't talk like that. Cal loves you for all the things you are. You're just feeling insecure and focusing on her as a result.

Mia: But it is totally normal to be jealous sometimes.

Gabi: You could put something horrible in her tea?

Nish: Oh yeah – defs normal. We've all been there.

Rosie: Including you??

Nish: Yeah I've been jealous. I was jealous this summer. I dealt with it.

Rosie: How?

Nish: Kept it in. Haven't mentioned anything about the

fact that after four years of a relationship she's off to hang out with slutty French artist girls. Easy.

Mia: Easy. Perhaps not healthy though?

Gabi: Hide some fish behind her radiator?

Chapter 11

Gabi messages me in the morning as I'm walking to work to check I knew she was joking and that I do know I have nothing to worry about. I reply saying, But I've already bought the fish for the radiator . . .

I wish I'd told them about Cal's midnight wandering. Or that when I texted him from outside the pub asking where he was he replied that he was at work. But then they might start thinking I do have something to worry about.

When I arrive at WANT Lifestyle Solutions, there is a commotion going on outside. A woman holding a box is being led away by security. And someone has graffitied the sign so it reads, *WANK Lifestyle Solutions*. Then I notice that the woman is also holding a can of spray paint. As I pass her she breaks one arm free from the security guard and points at me.

'They're all bastards – get out now!'

'Come on, Lorna,' says one of the guards. 'Don't make a scene.'

If I wasn't worried about starting work before, I am now. I Googled them and still couldn't work out what they actually do or what a 'Customer Satisfaction Enabling Communications Operative' is.

I stand in the lobby clutching the bag with my lunch in. When I woke up this morning the bed was empty and my heart sank, but when I went downstairs I found that Cal had got up before me to make me a packed lunch for my first day. He's put all my favourite things in – a salmon and cream cheese bagel, sweet and salty popcorn and a cookie. And on the way here I realised there was a note inside – a cartoon of a bagel holding a heart.

I sent a picture to the girls and they all replied saying VOM.

Even halfway through my induction I'm none the wiser about the job as I have to fill out a form titled *Contemporary Client Household Priorities for Optimum Lifestyle Satisfaction – And How We Can Help*.

It's only when I get taken into the main office and I see the rows of desks with people on the phone that it all makes sense.

'Hello?'

'Hi, is that Mrs Carson?'

'Who's this?'

'Hi, I'm Rosie. I'm just calling to talk to you about that accident you had.'

'I haven't had an accident.'

'Oh . . .' I start flicking through the script. 'Well, that's good.' I can't find the next bit. Then the whole script slides off the table and into the bin. The headset lead won't stretch far enough for me to get it. I think I have to ask them about pipes next? Or is it PPI?

'Never mind accidents. I'd like to ask you about pipes.'

'How did you get my number?'

I remember this bit in the script. It just says to distract them.

'Lovely weather today!'

'Eh?'

'Are you doing anything nice?'

'I want you to take me off your list. And never call me again.'

The slam of her hanging up makes me jump. I don't think I'm going to be very good at this job.

The other people working there seem to be able to keep people on the phone about ten times longer than me. And when they get hung up on they shrug, maybe chat for a while and then start on the next one.

Everyone else is older than me and there don't seem to be any other temps. I think that other people on the scheme must have said they wouldn't do call-centre work in their interview.

When I've been hung up on six more times and been told to 'fester in hell', I am thinking that they might have had the right idea.

The woman next to me is called Bruiser. Well, that's what

she tells me to call her. When I overhear her making a call I find out her real name is Patience. I think Bruiser suits her more. She looks a bit like a bulldog and has this menacing expression when she's making a call, while she is increasingly blunt and rude to the person on the other end of line. But her tactics seem to work. On the leaderboard by our desks she has way more hits than anyone else.

Everyone has their own column with a picture of their face at the bottom. Bruiser's looks like a picture of a murderer from the paper. As I'm only temporary, I have a generic photo. Only they'd run out of women, so mine is a picture of a man with a big cheesy grin that says 'Ian' at the bottom. I asked Clint, the Operatives Supervisor who is younger than most of the people he is supervising, why they didn't just get *Temp* printed on the bottom and he said that it would be too impersonal. Ian has no hits at the moment.

Also on our desk is a woman called Deborah, who is tiny and mousey and mutters rude comments about other people in the office when they go past. Then there's Georgie and Tina, who are the same shade of bright orange and spend most of the day chatting and then picking up the phone if Clint is around. Well, Georgie chats and Tina just repeats the last word of whatever Georgie's said and nods. Completing our table is Ron, a man in his fifties who doesn't say much but sighs when Clint walks past and says, 'Keep working hard, ladies.'

Chapter 12

Walking back through town (and checking around every two seconds that no one from the call centre is around) I phone Nish and tell her how awful it was, which she finds hilarious.

I hang up and music starts in my earphones again. I'm just about to call Cal to see if I will catch him before he goes out for his shift at the pub, when the music cuts out again and my phone starts ringing. It's Dad – the third time he's called since I got here.

In a weird way it made me feel more homesick to talk to him. So I kept the conversations as short as possible by inventing urgent things I had to go and do. (Being an awful liar the best I could come up with was 'I have to go and do some dusting'.) That reminded him that I hadn't sent him a picture of my room yet, so I said I would soon. Obviously by soon I meant never, because any picture of Cal's room would very clearly be Cal's room, unless my dad would believe that I would decorate my room with empty crisp packets and a poster of a girl in a bikini.

'Hi, Dad.'

'Hey, babes.'

Dad tries to be modern with his terms of affection. It doesn't seem to bother my sister (not much does) and I don't really have the heart to tell him I think it's weird. Like when he joined Twitter and kept tweeting me and I didn't tell him it was annoying, but just quietly blocked him.

'How was your first day in the hustle and bustle? The cut and thrust?'

I give quite a different account of my day to Dad than I did to Nish. I know he wants to hear that things are going well. It's probably something to do with him being a politician and always having to make out like everything is great. He asks me if I made lots of sales, so I say 'not lots' rather than saying 'none' and he says, 'Awesome – yeah, playing the long game.'

At least he's back to saying 'awesome' rather than 'amazeballs'. I think Mum had a word with him.

He's asking about the house just as I come out into that courtyard with the beautiful library building in it. I stop and look up at the window, but not because of the scenery this time. Because Cleo is sitting at one of the windows.

I peer in, trying to see what she's doing, while trying to answer my dad's questions.

Maybe I could ask Cleo if I could take a picture of her room and send that to Dad instead?

Would she find that weird, seeing as we've barely said two words to each other since I moved in? But then again she did go for a snog on the first day I met her, so she wouldn't be able to say I was forward.

She's reading. Which is hardly surprising, seeing as she's in a library. I don't know what I was expecting to catch her doing really. Then she looks up, straight at me.

I give a sort of yelp and Dad asks if I'm okay. How do I make it clear I wasn't just standing at the window staring at her? Especially as that is exactly what I was doing. I could pretend I was admiring the book she's reading?

I grin at her and then mime reading a book and then mime looking happy.

Which makes it look like first I was standing at the window staring at her and then now I am congratulating her on being able to read.

She raises her eyebrow at me and then does a sarcastic happy face. Then she picks up her phone and starts texting. I walk round to the front of the library as quickly as possible. When did miming ever turn out well? Dad's talking about Mum's military operation for redecorating the house so all I have to do is interested noises. Then I hear a burst of monkey noise, which I recognise immediately as Cal's text message tone. I look up towards the steps leading down from the entrance. Cal has just walked out of the library door.

Was he in there with her?

I tell Dad I have to go. He says he'll 'Facebook event' me to arrange my birthday meal and, instead of telling him to call me like a normal person, I tell him that would be nice. Music pumps into my earphones again and I go to turn it off before I call out to Cal so I don't accidentally shout really loudly. He's coming down the steps now and I'm walking parallel to him along the cobbles. Then a mad voice in my head tells me not to call out. It tells me to hide so I can see where he's going.

What's wrong with me? He has work tonight. That's where he's going.

But he also said he was going to be at home all day and he didn't mention any trips to the library with Cleo.

Chapter 13

I don't want to know how long it's been since someone cleaned this doorstep. I completely forgot Dan, Arlo and Simon were all going to the cinema. And I would have got back in time if I hadn't stopped to follow my own boyfriend to work and then waited outside to check he'd definitely gone in. Which he had.

Still, if he'd got me a key cut like he said he would then I wouldn't be locked out anyway.

I could walk back into town and pick up Cal's key from work. But he said he thinks Cleo will be back soon, so I should just wait. He said he'd just seen her because she left a book at home and he went to the library to give it to her before work. And I know I should be feeling guilty for even thinking I couldn't trust him, but if I'm honest I just felt relieved.

Does that make me a bad person?

'You're weird!'

I know! Wait a minute – what?

A cross-looking face is poking around the side of next door's porch. A little girl steps out. She looks about five or six and has red hair cut short with a fringe.

'Why are you sitting outside?' she says, eyeing me suspiciously.

'I'm locked out,' I reply, doing a mock-annoyed face.

'I thought you were a burglar,' she says, still frowning.

'No, I do live here.' I laugh. 'If I was a burglar I'd be trying to get in the window.'

'Is that what burglars do?' comes a horrified whisper from the door. The boy is smaller and looks younger than his sister, but has the same flame-red hair. He's peeping round the side of the porch so I can see only his eye and a bit of his face.

The girl gives a dramatic sigh and turns to the boy. 'Yeah! Everyone knows that!' Then she turns back to me. 'Rory is sensitive,' she explains.

I look round into their porch and wave. 'Hello, Rory,' I say, praying I haven't just given him a lifelong fear of people appearing at his window.

Further into the house I can see a man rummaging in a rucksack. He has a child's shoe in his mouth and looks quite flustered. He looks up, tries to speak and then takes the shoe out.

'Hope they aren't bothering you!' He grins.

'Oh, not at all!' I call back.

I've just been telling your children how to burgle a house, that's all.

'Well, *I* would strongly recommend that you . . .'

I lower my voice.

'That you listen to your son. He sounds very sensible.'

'That he is, love. He teaches maths.'

'Well, those are all the questions I have. Thank you so much for completing the survey, Mr Williams.'

'Oh no, thank you for calling, love. It gets quiet here sometimes.'

I hear the click of the receiver being hung up and then suddenly I am spun round away from my desk as someone grabs my chair.

'Rosie,' says Clint. 'How many hits have you had so far?'

'Um.' I pretend to be counting in my head.

Clint raises his eyebrows and looks over at the smiley picture of Ian on the wall.

'None,' I say.

'None,' he repeats. He shakes his head. And keeps on shaking it for about two minutes. 'Do you think that's good enough? Is that what we WANT?'

'Um, probably not. No. I'm sorry.'

He breathes in dramatically and holds his hand to his temple.

'Never,' he says, '*never* apologise. I have never apologised for anything in my life. If I ran over your grandmother I would not apologise, because apologising is saying you're not good enough. It's saying you can't. And "can't" is a filthy word here at WANT. What do you have to say to that, Rosie?'

My granny would make sure there were a lot of things he

couldn't do if he didn't apologise for running her over.

'Nothing. I mean, that sounds good.'

'Here at WANT we turn *No* into *Yes*.'

That sounds a bit rapey.

He carries on. 'And we turn "I'm sorry" into "I'm s . . . awesome".'

'How about "I'm selling"?' I suggest.

He nods at me approvingly. 'That's good,' he says. 'Maybe there is a future for you here after all.'

That might just be the most depressing thing I have ever heard.

'Write that down, Mary.' Clint gestures at the large lady in her fifties with pink cheeks who follows him around all day looking hunched and quite miserable, and she starts writing in her notebook.

'I'm watching you, Rosie,' Clint says. 'Shape up or get . . .' He waves his hand in the air. '. . . home. Shape up or go home.'

His assistant Mary is still hovering near my desk. She leans forward towards me.

'You know, his real name is Clive,' she whispers and then she scuttles off.

'Just quit,' Cal says as he does up his belt and then starts looking for his work T-shirt.

'I can't just quit,' I say.

'Why not? It's only a summer job.' He starts ruffling his hair up in the mirror, not that he ever styles it. He's just making it different versions of messy. 'Do something else,' he says.

I don't know why I can't face the idea of letting anyone down, even people I don't particularly care about and who aren't that fussed about me.

'I'm not a *quitter*, Cal,' I say with mock attitude.

He stops playing with his hair and I can see him looking at me strangely in the mirror.

'Maybe I can find a way to pay you to sit at the bar all day and keep me company,' he says, grabbing his phone and keys and putting them in his pockets. I shock myself as I realise I'd been willing him to forget his phone. So I could check it again. I'm shocked by how quickly it feels like a normal thing to do.

'I think those people are called escorts,' I say as he kisses me goodbye.

I spend the evening downstairs watching TV with the other housemates, except Cleo. Luckily they stay up until Cal gets back, so I don't have to face the temptation of the computer again.

I don't take in anything that's on the screen. Instead the text messages I read earlier flash in front of my eyes.

Cal: Thanks. You diamond! ☺

Cleo: No worries . . .

Chapter 16

'Hey, what shall we do tonight?' says Cal as soon as I walk through the door.

My heart sinks. I'm so tired I just want to lie down and do nothing. And I have my first Bright Sparx studying session tomorrow, so I should do some prep.

'I don't mind really. What do you want to do?'

He comes over and gives me a kiss on the lips. Then keeps hold of my head and looks at me.

'Are you okay?'

'I'm fine. Just quite tired.'

'Do you want to stay in my room and read tonight?'

I smile gratefully at him. 'I do!'

'Then I shall bring you tea.'

I throw my arms round him and hug him tight. 'I love you.'

'You love me when I bring you stuff,' he replies.

'Yes,' I say into his shoulder and he gives a small laugh.

I flop down onto the bed. Then I roll over and look at Mum's self-help book sitting on top of the Bright Sparx folder.

'I wish I'd brought some more books,' I say with a sigh.

'You can borrow one. Or ask Cleo – she's got loads in her room.'

He's on his way out of the door, but he turns back to see why I haven't answered.

'I said Cleo's got —'

'I know – I heard.'

The sharpness in my voice surprises both of us.

'I-I was just wondering when you've seen them.'

'What do you mean?' he half-laughs, but there's an air of suspicion in his tone.

'You've been in her room,' I say.

'Yeah, at some point. What's the problem?'

Again he is mostly baffled, but there's something else underneath it. Something harder and defiant. And not like Cal.

'There isn't a problem! It's fine. I was just asking.'

'Okay . . .' He frowns. And he goes downstairs to make the tea.

That's as bad-tempered as it gets between me and Cal. We never argue. Gabi and the others think it's unhealthy. Even Mia, who's more reserved than the other two, says she and Jamie like to have a good argument occasionally. It gets things out in the open.

So you don't bottle them up and think about them.

Constantly. When you're supposed to be concentrating on not screwing up an internship.

'What were you thanking her for?' I whisper to the empty room. However much I try to tell myself that I haven't actually found anything bad, really, and that it is my brain reading into it, questions just keep going round my head.

Why was he thanking her? If he was bringing her a book she left at home, why would *he* call *her* a diamond?

I feel like we're on the edge of something. For the first time with Cal I'm not worried about something small and stupid. It's bigger. Unless I'm mad and I've invented it all. I do feel like I've gone mad. All I'm thinking about is how I can get him to tell me about the messages without having to reveal that I've been looking at his phone.

There's a loud buzz from Cal's bedside table. That was a message.

I wait for a moment. Cal is talking to someone in the kitchen. So he won't be coming back up yet. My hand reaches out towards the table and I stay in exactly the same position, as if I'm trying to pretend that my hand is acting independently from me.

It's from Cleo.

`Fine, see you tonight.`

Everything else except the words of the text is blurry. I sit there, frozen, staring at them as if I'm willing them to fade, but they stare defiantly back out at me.

For some reason a line from a poem runs through my head. *While I debated what to do.*

It's from that poem by Robert Browning we did at

school. I think it's the guy realising his lover will leave him again in the morning, but for that moment he has her.

I have Cal now. If I can stay in this moment, while things are fine, and not try to find out, then nothing will change.

But I'll still be wondering. I've started noticing every detail of what he does when he's around her. When he was teasing her about her coffee addiction. Or the other night, when Arlo was asking her about the law course and she was saying how she might do a year abroad, and I saw that Cal was watching her, even when Arlo was speaking. And their eyes met for just a second. I'm sure they did. I didn't even know that Cleo did law. She's at Oxford and about to go into second year. I haven't made much of an effort to talk to her, I suppose. It would help if I wasn't so shy and she wasn't so terrifying.

I still don't know why she's not living with other Oxford people and has moved in with a load of Oxford Brookes people.

Unless she did already know Cal.

The guy in the poem decides to strangle the woman in the end.

I wish I could turn off my brain sometimes.

Chapter 17

'Hi, Mum.'

'Hi, Rose. Hang on, can you hold for a moment?'

'Oh, oka—'

Tinny classical music blasts into my ear and I wince. I always feel like I'm bothering Mum, which is ridiculous this time as she called *me*. But she did rescue me from a conversation with Cal, who caught up with me just as I was going out of the door. He was asking me if I was okay and he was sure something was up. I kept saying it was nothing and I was fine. I was on to the third time of saying it, sounding less and less convincing, when my phone rang. I showed him the screen.

'The Mother. So, I'd better . . .'

Cal nodded and gave one of his grins, although his eyes still looked worried.

'You'd tell me, though, if you weren't okay?'

I nodded vigorously and smiled as well. 'Yeah, yes. Of course. Anyway, I'd better go or I'll miss the call. Have a lovely day!'

I have a feeling that as I turned around we both stopped smiling.

Just as the music starts up for a third time there's a crackling sound and then Mum's voice is back.

'Rosie, hi.'

'Hey, Mum. How are you?'

'Internship going well?' Her voice is almost drowned out by the sound of a tannoy, so I think she must be on the train.

'It's . . . well, it's a bit rubbish, actually. I have to sell things and I'm awful at it.'

'Sorry, darling – signal's crap. What did you say?'

'It's fine, Mum.'

'You're doing well? Done all the reading?'

'Yeah . . .'

I stared blankly at some sheets from the folder last night, before pretending to go to sleep, so that I wouldn't confront Cal about Cleo.

'Jolly good,' she says brightly.

'How's everything with you?'

'All fine, all fine. The house is quieter.'

'Is it?'

'Yes,' she says. 'It's strange without you girls here.'

There's a pause.

'But we'll adapt! Anyway, my train's got in. Take care, darling. Keep working hard!'

And she's gone. I think that my mum might just have told me she misses me.

I look over at the Botanic Garden as I cross the bridge. On the river, one of the punting companies is setting up for the day. I left really early because the business school is a long walk from the house. Dan keeps offering to lend me his bike, but with my tendency to assume the worst I imagine cycling straight into a car, so I haven't taken him up on it.

On the other side of the road someone is standing outside the entrance to one of the colleges. I don't know why he's caught my eye and then I realise that he's standing completely still. Staring straight ahead through the big, wooden college doors and not moving a muscle. It reminds me a bit of one of those street performers, except he's not painted silver or anything and is just dressed in a pale blue shirt and black trousers.

His white-blond hair also makes him stand out and it's the only bit of him that's moving as it ruffles in the breeze.

It's a shock when he suddenly turns and starts walking up the street. He's going in the same direction as me, towards the town. We are walking parallel for a while and then he turns off into a coffee shop.

I overestimated the long walk and I'm the first to arrive. The building is like a really modern office with loads of glass. Nothing at all like the WANT Lifestyle Solutions offices, where the carpet is grey and the walls look like they are made of paper. The room I go into is a lecture theatre, so I sit down at the end of the row and put the self-help book Mum got me out on the desk.

'Excuse me, you're in my seat.'

'Oh, sorry.'

I start to gather up my stuff and look up to see where the voice came from. The guy with the white-blond hair and blue shirt from outside the college is standing there. He looks amused.

'I was joking – the room's empty,' he says.

'Oh!' I laugh and inwardly cringe.

The boy raises his eyebrows and in the pause before he speaks I realise that the shirt he's wearing is the same as one I bought Cal when we were going to one of my dad's functions.

When we were getting ready in my room he kept fiddling with the collar and I thought I'd got a size too small, but he said it was because he was nervous. You wouldn't have known that from the way he was when we got there. He seemed to be able to chat to anyone about anything. Dad would introduce him and go, 'This is my daughter's young man – training to be a lawyer.' And Cal would grin and shake their hands and launch straight into asking them what they did and what they were interested in. It was the complete opposite of how those things usually go, which is a stilted exchange where adults ask you what year you're in and how you're finding uni/sixth form and you say 'um' a lot and make out like the majority of your life is spent revising/playing an impressive musical instrument/charity work, and not messaging your friends/wasting time on the internet/watching entire boxsets and eating all the biscuits.

I saw him talking animatedly to some old ladies about *Midsomer Murders* and joking with a man whose job was importing wine about how 'it all tastes like wine really'. I even heard him defuse a fox-hunting debate by telling them all how he'd always wanted to raise a fox cub and puppy together so that they became best friends.

'He's pretty open, isn't he?' my sister said as we heard him telling someone that crisps make him gassy. She always made me stand with her at those things so she wouldn't have to talk to people and so I could cover for her when she snuck out for a cigarette.

'Yeah,' I said. 'Sometimes I think that when he's a lawyer he'll ruin cases by accidentally telling everyone he thinks his client probably did it!'

Cal glanced briefly in our direction and I wondered if he could hear us. Then someone dinged a glass for Dad to speak and the group Cal was talking to all stopped and turned round. I saw him fiddle with the neck of his shirt.

'Well, at least you'll know if he ever cheats on you. He'll probably just tell you!' muttered Poppy in my ear.

While I've been off in a daydream, the Cal Shirt Man has picked up Mum's business book off the table. He flicks through it and gives a look of disdain – first at the book and then at me.

I can't help noticing that the shirt fits him really well. His girlfriend must have got the right size.

'You think you can learn this stuff from a book?' he says.

I bloody hope so. If I have to rely on common sense or anything like that I'm screwed.

'I don't know,' I say, trying not to sound annoyed. Or worried. 'It might help.'

'It might,' he says. 'It probably won't. Can I borrow this?'

'Um,' I say, suddenly feeling protective of Mum's book, even if it is a bit awful.

'Thanks,' he says, turning and going down the steps to the front of the lecture hall.

When he gets there he looks back and laughs to see my face.

'Don't worry – I'll give it back.'

He sits on a chair in front of the first row. That's a bit keen. I deliberately sat back here to reduce the chance of being asked anything. He does seem confident, though – he must only be a year or two older than me, but the way he carries himself is like a proper adult.

The place gradually fills up. Everyone is either on their phones or glancing round the room suspiciously as if we are somehow in competition with each other.

There's a loud bang as someone sweeps through the door down at the front of the theatre. A woman with sharp cheekbones, red hair tied back in a bun and ever so slightly evil eyes is standing in front of us.

She announces that by the end of the course she will have turned us all into 'ball-crushers'. A few people shift uncomfortably in their seats.

As we file out of the room for coffee and biscuits I feel a tap on my shoulder. The Cal Shirt Man is holding out my book to me. My chest is gripped with hot embarrassment again as

I remember him being introduced about halfway through the talk as Martin Morton-Spitz, a mentor on the programme and a prodigy – already on the board of his father's sausage company aged only nineteen. He stood up, still holding the book, and pointed straight at me in the audience, saying that people shouldn't think they can just read all the books and get top marks in exams if they want to be successful in business. You need to get out there; interact with people; see what makes them tick. Then he chucked the book into a waste-paper basket in the corner of the room.

'Thanks,' I say now, taking it from his hand.

'Sorry for singling you out.' His eyes twinkle mischievously. 'But you seem like you spend too much time hiding in the background.'

'Thanks . . .' I say again. What I really want to tell him is that I would have preferred to stay hiding in the background and as far as possible from him.

'Perhaps I could make it up to you by taking you for a drink?'

He says it matter-of-factly – not like it would be in a film, with lots of 'undertones' and where it would be followed by a musical montage of us on various dates, laughing and having food fights and accidentally touching each other's hands.

I worry that I watch too many romantic comedies.

He says it like it's no big deal – like it would be unreasonable to say no. Which is what I have to say, isn't it?

'That would be great, but I can't – I'm only seventeen.'

'So?'

'Well, eighteen in a few weeks, but it's still illegal. We might get . . .'

I'm not sure where I'm going with this sentence. Saying we'll get arrested seems a bit extreme.

'. . . done.'

He laughs loudly. 'No, sorry. You're quite right. I wouldn't want to get *done*. Although I think that only happens to people in *Eastenders*. You know that it's possible to order non-alcoholic drinks?'

'Oh no, just gin for me.'

He smiles and then raises his eyebrows, waiting for my answer. I've just accidentally flirted with him. It's probably best if I just try and wrap the conversation up now.

'I can't – I'm going to a fancy-dress pub crawl thing tonight.'

A smile creeps into the corners of his mouth. 'What's the theme?'

'Animals.'

'I don't know whether to feel more sorry for myself or you.'

Chapter 18

Cal and I are getting our costumes ready in silence. We haven't spoken for fifteen minutes. I've been counting. Has he?

When I arrived home he was in his room, taking labels off the cow-print onesie. He asked me how the seminar went, but didn't wait for me to answer because he got distracted showing me the costume and asking how he should attach the udders. Then I started telling him about the smarmy guy on the course, but he was reading a message on his phone and clearly not listening, because he laughed and said, 'Oh my God!' before I'd got to the end of the story.

I asked him who he was texting and he said it was his brother. Apparently Max is going to drop in on the pub crawl. But he said it so quickly. Like he'd thought about what he'd say if I asked.

The pig and cow costumes seemed like a really funny idea when we planned them. But sitting here and getting them ready without talking seems to have sucked all the humour out of it. The only sound is my scissors chopping through the egg box to make the trotters. I have already made ears and a snout and attached them to a hair band. I also made a tail, but I don't think I'll wear it any more. I keep glancing up to look at him. And I think he's doing the same when I'm not looking.

Then we both glance over at the same time. He looks worried. But he turns it into an empty grin and so do I.

There's a pause and I feel the question creeping up my throat.

Are you sleeping with her?

The words start to form on my lips.

'Looking forward to the Run?' says Cal.

The Rugby Run is just the name they give to the team pub crawl, where they visit as many pubs as possible and as many colleges as they can charm their way into (very few).

'Yeah.' I nod. 'Well, I'm a bit worried about getting ID'd.'

'Nah, you'll be fine.' He waves his hand dismissively.

I get a flash of annoyance. He knows that if I get asked for ID I won't show them Poppy's passport, I'll just confess my age, apologise and leave. I don't really know why I bother bringing it out with me. The annoyance is accompanied by an image of Martin with his eyebrows raised saying, 'There are non-alcoholic drinks, you know.' I feel like saying that to Cal. But he never sees any obstacles to his fun. If I'm honest, I couldn't see Cal giving

106

a seminar on career-planning. Or anything serious.

I slice into the eggbox a bit more violently than I mean to and Cal looks up from adjusting his udders. We both do that empty smile again and Cal puts the radio on to fill the silence.

'Are you dressing up for the Rugby Run?' I ask Cleo as she leans against the doorframe outside her room, wearing possibly the tiniest shorts that have ever existed.

Cleo looks at my ears and snout. 'No . . .' she says.

I'm really glad I didn't put the tail on now.

Cal comes out of our room in his cow costume, complete with udders he made himself out of rubber gloves.

'Wow,' says Cleo. 'Lots of effort there, Cal.'

I hide my trotters behind my back.

'Oh yeah!' he says and then pretends to milk his udders at us.

'Come on!' says Simon from the door. He's dressed as an elephant, but has hung his trunk somewhere inappropriate.

Dan comes down the stairs from his room with pointy orange ears, whiskers, a tweed jacket and a farmer's cap.

'What's the theme?' Cleo laughs. 'Dickheads' day out?'

Dan stops on the landing. 'Actually, it's arrogance, so you don't even have to get changed. This,' he gestures to his costume, 'is Liv's favourite childhood book character.'

'I didn't know there was a children's book character called "ginger pervert in a coat",' says Cleo.

'Fantastic Mr Fox!' says Cal.

'Thank you,' says Dan pointedly.

'She'll love it, dude,' says Cal and starts down the stairs.

'Well, you losers have fun,' says Cleo.

'Aren't you coming?' says Cal, sounding disappointed, and the strangling feeling starts in my throat again. It's good I left the scissors in the bedroom.

'I'm ill,' Cleo calls down the stairs.

'Anything I can do to make you feel better?' Simon leans round the bannister and winks.

'I ate something bad and now I have the shits,' says Cleo, holding his gaze.

'Okay,' says Simon, but all the sound has gone out of his voice.

'Wait for me!' We hear footsteps crashing down the stairs and then Arlo appears on the landing with a kitchen roll holder sticking out from his forehead.

'I'm not even gonna,' says Cleo. She turns on her heel and walks into her room.

'What?' says Arlo. 'I'm a unicorn.'

Chapter 19

Pub one. Pimms.

I hide behind everyone and Cal gets my drink.

There is a lot of hugging and shouting and lifting people up as the rugby team reunite. I chat to Liv's friend, who I discover is called Emma, and tell her about my awful job. She replies that she's got a paid internship at a local newspaper that she really loves and it is exactly what she wants to do. Which is great.

I hear myself telling her how excited I am to be doing business studies at Manchester in September and how it will be great and set me up for a great job and then I'll have a great life. I say 'great' about ten times. I'm such a knob.

Pub two. Tequila shots.

I've never had them before, and it turns out that was

sensible because they are disgusting. I take a small sip and catch Dan's eye. We pretend to drink them and then run off and tip them into a plant pot.

I chat to Dan as we move on to the next place. He seems worried about whether I'm okay. Perhaps he heard me wittering on about total bollocks in the last pub.

Pub three. Beer.

Which I don't like, so I share Cal's. One of the guys turns up late and tells Cal it was a shame not to see him on the team last term, which is a bit weird. Maybe he's in a different team. Then he says, 'Where's your fit new housemate?'

Cal says, 'She's not here – she's ill.'

Before adding, 'But this is my fit new *room*mate, Rosie!' and giving me a squeeze, which he does a bit too enthusiastically.

Pub four. Glass of wine.

Dangerous. I find Emma again and start to tell her that I actually don't want to do business studies and that my mum is pressuring me into it because she's a CEO and I'm going to say more, but the call goes out that we are moving on and Emma seems quite glad to escape.

Pub five. Snakebite.

Some guy in a leather jacket knocks into me. I say sorry, even though it is me who now has cider and beer all over my arm. He sees my costume and says, 'Hmm, attractive.'

I step backwards into two other people and spend ages apologising to them as well.

Pub six. Shot, but I don't know what it is and it tastes horrible.

I can't find Cal for ages. It feels like ages. It may only be five minutes.

One of the rugby guys says he thinks Dan and Cal are outside, but I'm stopped from leaving by Simon, who wants me to follow a girl to the toilet and then talk about him loudly.

'On my own?'

'Take a friend!' he says and shoves me towards a group. Emma turns round, sees me and then quickly backs away.

I end up taking Liv into the toilets, but I think the girl has gone anyway. I think afterwards that I should have asked Liv how things are going with Dan.

Pub seven. Nothing.

Because I don't make it inside.

Dan and Cal have gone on ahead and are standing outside the door and talking in urgent whispers. I crouch behind a plant and listen.

Dan says, 'I get it, but you can't keep sneaking around behind Rosie's back.'

Cal says, 'I know. I just wasn't sure before. But I swear I'm going to tell her.'

Dear M,

It was nine o'clock when I heard the door go. I thought the pub crawl thing was meant to go on all night. I thought I had the house to myself and I'd be able to indulge in all the debauched habits I have now. Like talking to the cat and reading.

Don't laugh. It's easier this way. And all I read is the same book – the copy of On the Road *you gave me. You said the only people for you are the mad ones.*

In my quest to escape it all I probably should have gone to hitch-hike across the US as a penniless, drunken writer. Or taken mind-altering drugs in South America. Instead I went and rented a room in a house full of students.

If I told you I planned this all would you believe me? I tracked these people down. I've always envied them. But now I'm here, I can't join in.

I'd always wanted to be part of a gang. Then you came along. And I was part of us. Then you went. And here is this ready-made gang. Only now I'm more convinced than ever that I'm not capable of having friends.

I went to the top of the stairs to see which one it was that had interrupted my evening in.

Fantastic Mr Fox didn't look so fantastic. He grabbed his laptop from the living room and stomped into the kitchen. A few seconds later loud punk rock started blasting out. I walked in as he was putting on a T-shirt after taking off the costume.

I said, 'Wow, Kitchen Boy. If you keep up all this

brooding you're going to really change your nice-guy image.'

He took something from the fridge, slammed the door shut and grumped about not being in the mood tonight.

I walked further into the room and asked him what was wrong.

He thought, obviously deciding whether to share it with me of all people. Then he turned the music down and started talking.

Liv had gone off with some guy who apparently is horrible to her, but who she really likes. She told Dan she thinks he's lovely and they should be friends. And that's what happened with his last girlfriend. And the girl he met when he was travelling – they fell madly in love and then he found out she was still seeing her married, horrible ex.

He said that he always gets told he is 'such a nice guy' and 'such a good friend'. Like it's a good thing, but it hasn't been that good for him. Nice guys get dicked over and dickheads get the nice stuff, without even having to make any effort.

I came over and leant against the kitchen side next to him.

He was talking about this guy of Liv's again, and was like, what kind of bad boy actually wears a leather jacket? And said that he looked like such a tool.

I said I didn't know. And then I looked at his outfit. And so did he. And then we looked at each other. And burst out laughing.

He managed to get some words out between the laughs. He said he had dressed as a ginger pervert in a coat for her.

113

And then I laughed even more.

Dan made tea and asked if I wanted one. For once I decided to stick around. He went to the fridge to see if there was anything edible.

'What does cheese say to itself in the mirror?' he said, holding up a piece of cheese. 'Halloumi!'

I looked at him. 'Hello . . . me,' he explained. I told him that I got it. Then he looked at me in horror. And asked, 'Is it the jokes?'

I told him it wasn't. That the problem was that he was assuming people make intelligent, rational decisions. People are idiots. They'll make a decision for some reason they're not even really sure of and then make up a load of crap to make it sound like they thought it all out. 'There's no real reason these girls didn't pick you,' I said. 'They're idiots going through life and getting it completely wrong, like everyone else.'

Dan looked up at me with a serious expression. And asked if what I was saying was that a girl would be an idiot not to fancy him? I hit him on the arm and he grinned.

And then all the lights went out.

Dan said, 'Whoa! Do you think it's a power cut? Hey, my laptop's still working!'

I looked at him in disbelief (which he couldn't see obviously, because it was dark). So I told him that it was called a battery and reminded him he is doing a science degree. Then the laptop light went out.

He said his laptop battery is crap and actually he does engineering. (Surely that's worse?) We stood there in silence for a moment in the pitch black. Then I heard him move.

And after a pause I heard him speak. 'I'm just going to —'
Then he froze. And apologised.

I said, 'Yeah, that was my boob.'

I could almost see his horrified expression as he said that
he was really sorry, that he wasn't trying to grope me in the
dark, and that he was going to go and try to find the
switchboard.

Then silence again. And just the sound of us breathing.

I could feel he was only inches away from me.

I moved closer and I heard him move too. It felt like there
was some sort of electric field round us, playing over my skin
and intensifying the closer he got.

Closer again, and I could feel his leg between mine, just
touching. And then my hands were round his neck and his
were on my waist.

The force of the kiss moved me backwards and I felt the
kitchen table dig into my back. Dan's hands went under my
thighs and he lifted me up on to it.

You may wonder why I'm telling you all this.

I think it's because of the thrill I always got from sharing
things with you. When we'd walk through the city in the
darkness. Creep into a college and lie there under a looming
wall. In among the tradition and the ritual and the rules, we
shared something secret. No one saw us or heard the things
we told each other. We lay there looking up and I turned to
you and you turned to me. And I told you how I was always
numb and I'd never felt it. You reached out and drew me in
and unlocked it all. So that's why I'm telling you this. I want

to feel that again.

Or maybe I'm trying to make you jealous.

I curled my legs around Dan's back to pull him against me. His hands ran up my sides and over my breasts. Everywhere I couldn't feel him ached for that firmness. The contact. That thing I'd missed. I pulled at his T-shirt and he took it off, while I took off my top. I heard his intake of breath as he put his hands on me again and felt bare skin.

And then the light came on. And we froze.

He looked into my eyes, his chest rising and falling against me. His hand in my hair.

I said that I hadn't done this before.

When the clothes went back on we went into the sitting room. We lay on the sofa. We'd been planning to watch a film but the talking overtook us and we never got past the menu screen.

He asked me about the guy I brought back to my room the other night. I stared at him. He'd believed that I'd brought home some pervy businessman. I corrected him – it had in fact been a wild night in talking to the cat.

He cracked up. I thought I'd feel pathetic admitting something like that. But I started laughing too. Then Dan shifted round to look at me and said, 'So you've never slept with anyone?'

You can imagine what went through my head then.

Lying on the grass. Gripping your hand to me. Creeping up the winding staircase and along the corridor. Fumbling with the keys for what felt like an age. You pushing me up against the door. And then, finally.

116

I said no, I haven't slept with anyone. I said it looking up at the ceiling, because I knew I'd give something away if I met his eye. Even though it had turned into some big confession-fest, I still couldn't talk about you. Then I told him to keep that to himself – that I had got a reputation to keep up.

I could feel him looking at me.

'Have you ever been in love?'

It caught me off guard and I found myself answering before I could think about it. I said yes.

He asked me if I was talking about Jamie.

I didn't say anything. I couldn't. I turned away from him. Because it strangles me, thinking about it.

I shouldn't have told you that – you'll get arrogant.

He checked himself, sensing that maybe he'd gone too far, and apologised. He then asked if I would rather be talking to the cat?

The grip relaxed slightly and I let myself laugh. And at that moment the cat launched itself onto the sofa and did its usual thing of sitting on my chest. Practically on my throat.

He said he knew that I would give in to the cat-love eventually.

I stroked its ear and said, 'Well, you wouldn't bugger off, would you, Ma— Nigel?'

I froze. Dan didn't notice and he carried on talking. But I couldn't hear anything. It's the first time since it happened that I nearly said your name.

Love you.

Cleo x

Chapter 20

Pub eight. Something blue?

'Max!'

I launch myself at him, knocking a few people out of the way. Spend a while apologising to them, obviously.

'Hello!' he says.

I managed to avoid Cal the whole walk over and I get the impression he's not trying to find me.

The bar is busy, so it is hard to hear everything Max says. And I think that the alcohol might be blocking up my ears. Can that happen? Max tells me he was on his way from a breakdancing battle and driving past Oxford, so Cal persuaded him to stop by. I say how Gabi is always getting us to watch videos of him dancing. He says she's always embarrassing him, but he looks pleased.

I tell him he should do some of his moves in the pub and

he refuses. I keep saying it. Until it becomes awkward.

I tell him that a really nice thing about going out with Cal is that I've got to know Max better. He says he likes it too.

I tell him that he should get back together properly with Gabi. He says it's up to her really.

I tell him that I think Cal is cheating on me and what I heard him say to Dan and that I've read his phone and looked on his computer. He doesn't really get a chance to say anything, because I carry on talking.

I tell him about the Spankathon video.

Suddenly Max's face comes into focus. He's holding a bottle of beer and he's saying, 'You shouldn't be selling me this.'

I look at him, confused. I say, 'I'm not selling it to you, Max, the people at the bar are.'

I can't find him after that.

Pub nine. Nothing (cannot find the bar, or anyone I know, or my purse).

Realise that Max said, 'You shouldn't be *telling* me this.' Directed to the next pub by strange man in robes who might be in a cult. Go into the toilets to collect my thoughts and decide what to do, but instead I am sick.

Pub ten. Water.

Fed to me by a kindly stranger after I am found face down in another toilet.

Pub eleven. Water/beer.

Realise kindly stranger was Arlo. He walked me to the next place and because I obviously have some sort of death wish I steal his drink when he's not looking.

Pub thirteen. Sip of something horrible from a hip flask.

Fed to me by an old man after I tell him I am looking for my boyfriend who has left me for a whore. He then tells me I have missed pub twelve. Have an epiphany as I walk back up the road to find pub twelve and realise that the strange man in robes was Simon in his elephant suit.

Pub twelve. Nothing.

Barman asks for ID and I run away. I actually run.

Pub fourteen. Nothing.

Find everyone else and am briefly deliriously happy, but soon go back to feeling sick. Decide alcohol is a terrible thing. Worse than drugs. Tell lots of people this. Decide I am going to find Cal and sort this out once and for all.

Pub fifteen. Nothing.

The pub Cal works in. I march up to him at the bar. He ushers me outside and we end up walking out of the little alleyway the pub is in to the road. Soon the walls of the colleges on Broad Street are looming up around us. It's probably the most wide open, public place we could be. Cars and bicycles whiz past and people shout out things to us. Some ask if we're okay. Which I guess you would do if you saw a couple screaming and crying at each other.

And if that couple were dressed as a pig and a cow.

Botanic Garden.

Sitting on our bench – not quite sure how we got in here, but I think a hedge was involved. Both fully clothed. I think we just broke up.

Chapter 21

'Hello?'

'Good morning, is that Mrs . . .'

That can't be right.

'Cockbum?'

Oh no, wait, that's an 'rn', not an 'm'. My tired eyes went blurry and now I've just called someone Mrs Cockbum.

'Cockburn?'

'It's pronounced Co-burn.'

How?

'Oh, I do apologise, Mrs Co-burn. I was wondering if you had two minutes to —'

Slam.

My hand is shaking as I take a sip from my glass of water. I feel completely hollow. No sleep in two days hasn't helped. But it was the sober, quiet argument that drained me even more than the screaming, drunken one.

It came the day after. After Cal had slept in Dan's room, because Dan was asleep on the sofa. I passed out and relived our fight (or what I could remember) over and over again in horrible, vivid dreams. He walked in in the morning, looking pale and tired, not wanting to look me in the eye.

Because our fight didn't get rid of the problems. It made them real and unavoidable.

'Hello?'

'Good morning. Is that Mr Beard?'

'This is *Mrs* Beard.'

'Oh! I do ap—'

Slam.

We both had our things. The things that kept rearing up and we couldn't get past. His was that I could think he was the kind of person to cheat on me. Mine was that all his friends knew that he was possibly getting kicked off his course. Everyone knew, except me.

'Who's this?'

'My name is Rosie and I'm calling fr—'

Slam.

He hadn't intended to confide in Cleo, apparently. She'd found him downstairs in the middle of the night, working on an essay. They'd told him he could stay on the course if he handed in three essays and resat one of the exams. Cleo had managed to persuade some second year to give her all his essays last year, so she offered to help Cal.

But, I told him, surely he'd know that sneaking into her room at night would look dodgy. The way he 'Oh' when I said that was like it hadn't even occurred to him. That's the biggest difference between us – he doesn't think. I think too much.

'Why didn't you tell me?' I said. Even though I knew what he was going to say.

He said he didn't want to disappoint me. He talked about when I introduced him to my parents and went on about how he was going to be a lawyer. And how I always told him I was proud of him. I wanted him to shut up. He was taking lovely moments between us – stuff that I used to think of and smile – and turning them sour.

I told him to shut up.

And that he was wrong. I'm not the sort of person who would care if he fails. I just want him to be happy. He looked at me with this tired, sad face. A face that was nothing like him.

'I'm not going to do my exam. I'm going to drop out.'

I met his eyes.

'That's fine,' I said. My voice came out high and tight.

'See. You can't hide it. You're disappointed in me. You don't want to be with a dropout.'

He was kneeling so close to me. My heart ached so much it stung. All I wanted to do was reach out and hug him, but I couldn't. Because when he'd said it, a flash of disappointment went through me.

He thinks I'm cold and unfeeling.

Am I?

He stood up.

'I can't deal with someone looking at me like that, sorry.'

I was angry then. He'd decided for me – he hadn't given me the chance to be supportive. And I was angry about the voice in me that was wishing he'd stay on the course. I wanted to lash out – think of something to say that wouldn't let him make me the bad person and then just walk off.

'Maybe if you'd spent less time watching porn and more time doing your work then this wouldn't have happened.'

He span back round and stared at me. 'What?!' he said, almost laughing.

'I saw – on your computer.'

He frowned, looking less confused, but still confused. Okay, it had been one video. But still.

'Why were you on there? You have your own.'

'What? I . . .'

'Were you checking up on me there as well? Like on the phone?'

'I don't think that's the point, Cal.'

He ruffled his hair in frustration and sighed. Then looked around the room, trying to work out what to say. The seconds dragged out painfully.

'I feel I have to be perfect for you,' he said eventually.

'I don't want – I never said that.'

'No, but it's you. You have all these . . . high standards and you beat yourself up if you think you're not meeting them. Why wouldn't you have them for the person you're with?'

I couldn't speak. It felt like his words were ramming into my chest and everything was blocked by this confused ball of feeling that I couldn't work out. Pity that he felt like that and outrage that he'd got me wrong and a cold guilty feeling that he'd got me right.

He swallowed. 'Maybe we should talk later. When it's not so . . . I don't know. I'm sorry, Rosie.'

Then he walked out of the door and I was alone in his room again.

I can't bring myself to make another call. The headset suddenly feels tight and like it's pinching my head. I pull it down so it's round my neck. Quite vigorously, apparently, because Bruiser turns round.

'You okay?' she grunts.

Up till now I'd managed to keep it in. Even when the Noah and the Whale song came on shuffle when I was walking to work. And when one of the people I called said nonsense words until I hung up, which is what Cal always does to cold callers. And when Georgie and Tina spoke for ages about Tina moving in with her boyfriend.

But 'Are you okay?' always gets me.

I try to nod and tell her I'm fine, but my voice goes wobbly and all the sadness wells up everywhere. And soon I'm sobbing noisily at my desk. The kind of sobbing where you can't control your breathing and you make loads of weird gulpy sounds and people look over to find out how a dying pig managed to get into the office.

Everyone on my table looks up. And, between sobs, I start to explain. Georgie and Tina come over and Georgie says it's Cal's loss and he's obviously a total knobhead. Tina says 'Knobhead' and nods. Ron, the only man on our table, gets me some Maltesers from the vending machine because he says his wife likes to eat chocolate when she cries. Then Bruiser pats me on the back in what is meant to be a reassuring way and I fall off my chair. Deborah the office gossip puts her head over my computer and says that from what she could see on Facebook Cal was clearly a wrong 'un and was putting on weight.

I'm so grateful for how nice everyone's being that I don't even think about the fact that I'm not friends with Deborah on Facebook till later.

I don't tell them any of the details of it. I just try to smile and nod and say thank you over the sob sounds. And they tell me I can do better and all men are bastards, but it doesn't matter what they say really, I just want it to carry on so I don't have to go back to thinking about it. Slowly my breathing returns to normal and the tears stop flowing. And then Clint comes over. He puts his hand over mine in a slightly creepy way.

'Rosie,' he says. 'No one likes failing. Especially failing in the arena of love. But look on the bright side. You're quite an attractive girl. I probably would. And I don't say that lightly.'

And I burst into tears again.

Chapter 22

I walk into the pub and Cal lifts his head from the pit of depression he's been in all day. He stands up and looks at me, his eyes sparkling because he has also been crying noisily in front of all his colleagues all day. Then he starts walking towards me. By a coincidence, a love song has started playing on the pub sound system. I'd like to pretend it's something cool and indie, but actually it's Love Story *by Taylor Swift. When he reaches me I start trying to tell him how I want us to sort everything out and he puts his finger gently on my lips and says, 'Shh. I love you. Nothing else matters.' Then he grabs the back of my head and kisses me (just at the bit in the song when the key changes) and everyone applauds. I look at the crowd on the patio and realise all our friends and my parents are there. Mum smiles at me and then she shouts, 'Get out of the way!'*

Wait a minute.

There's a flash of black and a shrill, high-pitched bell rings out. I jump back onto the pavement and the bike whizzes past, missing me by inches. I was in a complete daze, standing at the crossroads at the top of Broad Street where my fight with Cal started. It's also next to Cal's work and I know he finishes his shift soon.

The same scenarios have been playing in my head on a loop while I've wandered aimlessly around town for the two hours since I left work.

1. I walk into the pub and find crying Cal. Then, kissing, applause and Taylor Swift.

2. I walk into the pub and instead of Cal I find Cleo. She tells me Cal has left to catch a plane to France, not because he doesn't love me, but because he thinks I don't love him and it is too painful to stay. Cleo puts her hand on my arm and tells me to go because I might still catch him. I turn and run and soon I am approaching the airport barrier. (Conveniently the imaginary airport is running distance from the pub.) I stop Cal just as he is about to go through the gate (after having leapt over a security barrier like the little boy in *Love, Actually*). Then, kissing, applause and Taylor Swift.

3. I don't go to the pub, but instead leave a note for Cal telling him I've gone to the Bright Sparx networking event (beautifully written with the fountain pen I happened to have in my bag). Cal comes looking for me and arrives at the party to see me at the centre of a group of people telling a hilarious story. He realises what he's missing and then kissing, applause, Taylor Swift.

None of this is actually helping me decide what to do. But while I've been thinking it, my feet have walked me to the alleyway that leads to Cal's pub.

The road has all these lovely little houses on it, painted different colours like pink and blue and yellow and all of them with beams on the ceilings. Cal and I always said that when we lived together it would be a place like the ones on this road.

I can't believe that we'd talked about living together and now I can't even walk up to him and speak to him. How can you think of living with someone who you aren't even honest with? And who isn't honest with you? I feel hollow as I wonder if the whole time we've just been telling each other what we think the other one wants to hear.

Next to the pub is a little, old-fashioned inn where we stayed once. Most people would think it was ridiculous to stay somewhere right by where you work, but Cal thought it was brilliant. He phoned me to tell me that it had taken exactly twenty steps for him to get to work. Then he snuck back to see me on his break. Then phoned me to say he'd made it back in nineteen.

I can't help smiling, but just as I am picturing him, I hear him. Laughing. I stop in the tiny passageway next to the pub.

Cautiously, I edge forward so that I can peep round the wall. A big group of people are sitting round a table on the outside patio and playing cards. Cal's laugh rings out again.

As I wait in the passageway, a new and quite different scenario starts playing in my head.

4. I walk out on to the pub patio and find Cal playing cards with all his friends. His eyes are completely dry, because all the fun he's been having hasn't left any time for noisy crying. He tells me I shouldn't have come and that I should move out of the house and go home. But first he is going to kiss all of his female colleagues and make me watch.

I turn around and walk away.

Chapter 23

Quite a few students are here already. The networking event is at one of the Oxford colleges. It's one that is hidden away from the road and is quite small compared to the other ones I've seen, but still with the old-looking sandstone buildings set round a quad. Flowers and vines creeping up the walls make it seem less austere than some of the others and it must be one of the more relaxed ones because we are allowed on the grass. Long tables of drinks are laid out on the quad and waiters with trays of food are dotted around. The scary red-headed ball-crusher woman who runs the course is here.

I go over to one of the long tables to pick up my name badge. As I sign in, I take a deep breath. I've been thinking so much about this being something that could distract me from thinking about Cal, I've forgotten I will need to 'network'. There are going to be people from local businesses here to give us advice and, in the words of the course leader woman, 'judge us'.

As I think that, I hear her voice ring out over the quad.

'Good to see you, Steve. We weren't sure if you would make it.'

I turn back towards the main doors and see the man who lives next door to Cal, with Rory trotting along beside him and Rose running full pelt onto the grass.

'It's the BURGLAR GIRL!' she shouts as she sees me.

Heads turn around the quad.

'I was locked out,' I say and I get a few wary looks before people return to their conversations.

Steve waves apologetically as he walks over towards the woman. Rose runs towards me and Steve looks like he thinks about stopping her for a second and then decides to let her go. She's sprinting and her hair is sticking up all around her head like a fiery halo. I think she might be about to jump on me, but then she suddenly stops dead.

'Hello.'

'Hi, Rose. How are you?'

She starts telling me about the summer holidays club she is going to and how it was 'Pirate and Princess Dress-up Day' last week, but she didn't want to go as a princess.

'Oh, cool. Did you go as a pirate, then?'

'No, a bear.'

Her father calls over to her to come and have some squash, but at the same time he's explaining to Ball Crusher that he can't stay long.

'I couldn't find a babysitter,' he says. 'And I don't want

these two terrorising you the whole evening.'

I look down at Rory, clinging to his dad's leg and staring up with his big eyes. I can't really imagine him terrorising anyone if I'm honest. Rose, however, has picked up a piece of gravel and looks like she might be about to carefully drop it in the woman's drink, which she's left on one of the tables.

'Hey, Rose,' I say quickly. 'Why don't you tell me about being a bear?'

She comes over and starts doing loud bear impressions, but at least the course leader won't be choking on any stones.

The networking goes on all around me and I'm deep in conversation with a five-year-old. Even Rory, who is sitting obediently on a wall and reading a book, comes up to show me a picture of a cat and tells me his dad is letting them get a kitten soon. Steve might have a job getting them to agree on a name, seeing as Rory wants to call it Oliver, while Rose prefers the name Big Bum.

Steve finishes talking to the course leader and chats to me. It turns out that he is an economics lecturer at this college. And he's a single parent since his wife died two years ago, which is why they've downsized into the house next to Cal. There's one of those awful pauses that always happens when someone tells you something like that and you don't know how to react. But he fills the moment by thanking me for watching over the kids so he could at least talk to a few students.

It's at that moment that he remembers that I am one of those students and he asks me how the placement is going.

The conversation shifts to the surface and I go into 'trying to impress people' mode. I'm like a talking CV, and I don't think he buys it for a second.

'I would never have made a salesman,' he says with an easy grin, running his hand through his thinning hair. 'But it's certainly exciting seeing young people going out there and doing things and thinking that maybe you had a part to play in getting them to question things and develop their ideas – if that doesn't sound horribly cheesy.'

It doesn't. No one's ever put it like that before. I've always had in my head that I have to 'succeed', without thinking about what that actually means.

I'm left thinking about that as the family leave. Then it's like someone turns the volume up again and I'm aware of all the groups standing round chatting.

'Deep in thought?' comes a voice from behind me.

Standing there and holding out a glass of orange juice to me is the mentor, Martin. In another smart shirt and light brown trousers. It's like he's already comfortable with being an adult, not trying to seem grown-up while secretly worrying that someone will soon realise that he's not a proper person.

'Thank you,' I say and he does a jokey clink of glasses with me.

'And how was the animal pub crawl?' he says. 'As delightful as I imagine it?'

'It was great,' I say.

If your idea of great is feeling very ill and breaking up with your boyfriend while dressed as a pig.

He raises a sceptical eyebrow. 'I'm glad it was worth passing up my offer of a drink.'

'They were offering me lots of drinks,' I say. 'I went for the better deal.'

He laughs. 'You're learning.'

A group of girls has managed to sidle up to us from all the way over on the other side of the quad. One of them expertly moves to pick up a leaflet on the table behind Martin and uses it as an 'in' to introduce herself.

Now it's a group of us all talking. Which usually would mean I'm completely silent, thinking of jokey comments and stories to say, running them through my head, deciding they're too inane/weird, not saying them, then having someone else say something really similar and wishing I had said them first. I end up continually saying 'Me too' and nodding, so that in the end they probably decide that I don't have my own brain or life.

But this time Martin is running things. He directs the conversation and brings me in. I even get a laugh when I tell them some of the names of people I've had to phone up on the placement. For half an hour I feel like a different person. And even though I know it's all false and I'm playing a role, I can almost distract myself from everything else.

I find myself wishing Cal could see me.

Especially when Martin takes us on a tour of the college and he puts his hand on the small of my back. Even though I know the spectacle of a group of girls all competing for some suave guy's attention is pretty cringe. I try to ignore the mental image of my friends all making vom faces. He shows us the amazing bedroom he'll be in next year because he got a first. It has its own sitting room.

I end up being at the college right till the end and all the tables are being cleared away. So I managed a networking event. I swapped numbers with some people (one girl even had business cards). I was so positive about the call-centre job that for a moment even I forgot how awful I am at it. I wonder if that makes me one of the young people going out into the world and getting what I want that Steve was talking about. What he said is nagging at me for some reason.

I haven't looked at my phone all evening – highly unusual behaviour for me. When I take it out there's a string of texts, all from Cal.

```
This is rubbish, isn't it? I think we
should go back to never fighting! Been so
sad all day x

Just got out of work — had to stay for
leaving party — ugh! Do you want to meet
up? I've missed you today x

Sorry — remembered you have that drinks
thing! I could come there or we could meet
after? x

Guess that's a no . . .
```

Chapter 24

I wake up in Cal's bed alone.

When I got in last night he was still up, playing on the Xbox in the front room. I told him I hadn't got his messages until really late and he said it didn't matter. I said there wasn't any signal in the college and he said it was fine.

It turns out he did go to find me and 'a boy in a bow tie' told him I was in some guy's bedroom.

When I told him that wasn't what it sounded like, his reply was that he would crash in Dan's room and I could have his. I don't know if he meant just for the night or for the rest of the summer.

The bed feels huge without him in it. I look over at the door and I'm taken back to the moment I met Cal. It was at this house party last summer. Max and Gabi had broken up a couple of weeks before but, as she was determined that they were going to stay friends, she said that nothing should change.

I'd got a bit more tipsy than I intended, which happens sometimes when I'm nervous and in large groups of people. Nish decided it was time to put me to bed when she found me dancing to no music in the kitchen.

I slept soundly for a few hours and then was woken up by someone crashing through the door.

He was naked, wearing a Santa hat and holding a cup of tea.

I sat up in the bed.

'Um . . .'

He jumped about a metre in the air and flung tea everywhere.

'Oh, hello! How are you?' Then he winced as some tea had obviously gone somewhere unusual.

'Good . . . thanks.' I felt a bit delirious from being woken up.

And I could not stop staring at his willy. It was just there. Being a willy. While he was asking how I was, like everything was perfectly normal.

He followed my eyeline.

'We were doing naked running and I came in for a tea break.'

'Right.' I nodded.

He put the Santa hat over it and grinned at me. 'Would you like some tea?'

'Okay,' I said.

'You're Gabi's friend, aren't you? Rosie?'

I nodded. 'You're Max's brother, right?'

'That's right, I'm Cal.' He held his hand out to shake mine and the Santa hat fell off.

'I should find something less flimsy,' he said and started scanning the floor. 'Ah!' he said and picked up a scarf that was hanging on the inside of the door. He wrapped it round himself and tied it in a knot. 'How's this?'

'It . . . looks a bit like a nappy,' I said.

And we both started laughing.

An hour later I was still under the duvet with my legs pulled up to my chin. We'd been talking about random stuff like cheese and animals and what our ideal superpower would be.

I looked at him and tried to work out what it was I liked about him. The messy hair was just as messy then, in complete contrast to his brother, who used to gel his to within an inch of its life. He was well built, like a rugby player, I thought, but one who enjoys his food. He had sideburns and stubble and a big open grin. All his expressions seemed a bit exaggerated, like when he was talking enthusiastically about something his eyebrows curled right upwards and his eyes were all wide and sparkly. Then I knew what it was I liked. It was all of him.

'You got any plans for the weekend?' said Cal, lying back on the bed in his scarf nappy.

'No, why?' I said.

He turned his head and gave me a grin. 'I want to take you out of course!'

* * *

140

I'm still watching the door. But no one comes crashing in. I've been going over what I want to say – to let him know that I did want to see him last night. I lie there, poised and listening, until I hear him coming down the stairs from Dan's room. Then I leap out of the bed and walk out on to the landing.

He stops on the bottom step, his hair sticking up at different angles and his eyebrows knitted in a sleepy frown. He's wearing his T-shirt with the cartoon penguin on and boxers and socks, which I always mock him for wearing in bed.

'Hey,' he smiles.

'Hi,' I say.

This confused, unspoken surge of feeling shoots between us. It's horrible and lovely seeing each other at the same time.

'How are you?' he says.

'Fine, thanks. How are you?'

My throat feels all tight. It's so weird, speaking in this polite way to him. And not saying anything that means anything.

'Yeah, good. Are you off to work?' Cal says, knowing that I am.

I nod. There's silence and Cal swallows and fiddles with the bannister.

'Got anything planned for the weekend?'

'Nope.' My eyes fill with tears and I blink to try and make them go away.

I want him to ask me to do something.

Cal sees the tears in my eyes and frowns. He looks down and I see his hand move forward. A jolt goes through me as I think he's going to reach out and hug me.

But he points sideways at his bedroom door.

'I was just going to get some stuff.'

'Oh, go ahead,' I say.

'Not if you're still —'

'No, it's fine.'

'You sure? I don't mind waiting.'

'No, no. You go ahead.'

As he walks into his room, he accidentally brushes past me and our hands knock together. We both apologise. Now I really understand what the phrase 'painfully nice' means.

Rosie has joined the conversation.

Gabi: ROSE! How the devil are you? I have everyone in my bedroom. We are all on our phones. My sister said we were losers, so I kicked her.

Mia: How was the crazy pub crawl?

Gabi: Yeah can't believe you were going to twenty million pubs, you nutter! Did you find me a fancy man?

Nish: Good to know you're not dead. After I spoke to you I was a bit worried.

Rosie: Hey ☺ It was good thanks! I spoke to you??

Gabi: Good?! That's all I'm getting? I want the goss!

Nish: Yep, you called. You made no sense.

Gabi: Max is here – he says he saw you!

Rosie: What did he say?

Mia: That you tried to touch him.

Gabi: LOL. Hands off.

Rosie: LOL

Gabi: Nah he just says you weren't making any sense. There was really no goss? What about Cleo? Or Handsome Dan?

Mia: Gabi!

Gabi: Oh let it go, he's not in your love triangle any more!

Mia: True. I've had my Twilight moment.

Rosie: Cleo didn't go and Dan left early. Sorry – there was a distinct lack of goss! ☹ How have you guys been?

Chapter 25

I sit curled up on the sofa on Saturday morning. Cal and I are still being ridiculously polite to each other and haven't sorted anything out. Dan's been nice and friendly, but there's only so much I can say to him seeing as he's Cal's friend and they must have been talking about it.

I chatted to Arlo for ages about *The Lord of the Rings*, but when I said something about Cal loving the films and he thought I might start talking about the break-up he literally ran out of the room.

Cleo's not much to be seen, as usual. I should really go and tell her I'm sorry that I assumed she was an evil boyfriend-stealer. I'm not sure how much she knows about my fight with Cal, but she must have worked out it had something to do with the late-night room visits. But she isn't the easiest person to talk to and I don't find it easy to talk –

so in our different ways we are equally socially rubbish.

The only thing that's different, apart from me and Cal, is that Dan and Cleo seem to be getting on better.

I just think that if I'm here we'll have to sort it out. But at the same time I can't face it. I'm never the one who makes decisions. Not even what film we watch or what flavour ice cream we should get. Cal always chooses.

I keep trying to watch films or episodes of TV programmes to occupy my brain, but I just stare blankly at the screen and pay no attention. I went to buy a book after work, but everything I picked up seemed to be about stupidly happy couples being in love and happy and making me feel like being sick.

I notice a book lying next to the sofa and I pick it up. *On the Road* by Jack Kerouac. I don't think Jack and his friends were too in love and happy and vomitty. They were the ones who were all depressed and thought life was pointless, weren't they? Maybe this will help.

I open it and see that someone's written on the first page.
To my mad one. Love M x
Then I'm distracted by a message on my phone.
An invitation.

Dear M,

I got taken out on a day trip today. I kid you not. I'm being socialised against my will.

I could hear them all talking about it in the kitchen. I don't think they realise that the sound carries up to my room. And I am perfectly aware that they're all discussing how I need to get out of the house, like some sad, elderly relative.

Bloody Dan, I was thinking. He was supposedly my ally now, and he seemed the most determined that I really should be best friends with them all.

I heard them coming up the stairs and wondered how easy it would be to climb out of the window. The cat leapt onto the sill and eased itself inside through the gap, just to rub it in my face. I could probably get down the drainpipe and then onto the kitchen windowsill and into the back garden without too much of a problem.

Bit extreme?

The knock at the door was an awkward, jaunty rhythm so I knew it was Arlo.

I didn't say anything and the next one was three loud raps on the wood. Dan. It was more difficult to ignore.

I shouted out, 'What?', the door opened and they all filed in. I asked them what they wanted while pretending to be on my phone.

Arlo cleared his throat and said that this was an intervention. Or to put it more accurately a friend-tervention. (I'd heard him asking them downstairs if he could call it that. They'd said no.)

Cal interrupted and pointed at me and said they were taking me out. No arguments. And no more staying in your room like a sad case.

I half laughed and said that I'm not lonely. And then I realised that no one had mentioned being lonely. There was a moment of stand-off and I looked at Dan. Something strong was glinting in his eyes. It was easier when he didn't like me. Then the cat walked over, stretched and sat at Dan's feet, joining their side.

I sighed, stood up and admitted defeat. When I asked where I was being taken Cal tapped the side of his nose and said, 'Ah!' Then he put his arms round Simon and Arlo and shouted, 'Come on, guys. Day trip!' Arlo winced, as Cal was obviously gripping his shoulder tighter than was comfortable. But Cal was oblivious and pretty much danced them out of the room. He's very much over-compensating at the moment. But you either go one way or the other, don't you? Strangely, I think Rosie and I are similar. Hiding.

Dan hadn't gone with the others. He turned to me as we left the room and told me to bring sensible shoes, and I told him to fuck off. It was Arlo and Simon's idea, he said. I was seriously surprised that Simon would have anything to do with it and that must have shown in my face because Dan said that deep down Simon just wants to be a good friend.

We'd got to the bottom of the stairs by then and Simon was in the front room, slipping a pair of knickers off the clothes horse and into his pocket.

'Deep, deep down,' said Dan.

At the bottom of the stairs we saw Cal talking to Rosie. Dan and I caught each other's eye as Cal invited Rosie out with us. He said it casually, like she's just another housemate, not his possibly-broken-up-with girlfriend (long story — no one in the house has any idea what is going on), but he couldn't hide the way his shoulders dropped in disappointment when she said no. Something about meeting some friends for lunch. He said he didn't know the girls were coming up. She said they weren't, that it was friends from her summer course, and then she started rambling about how she didn't want to go really, but she'd said she would and she probably should if she wants to do well at the course etc, etc. I get the impression Rosie spends a lot of time going to things she doesn't want to. But then I'm not really one to talk, considering I allowed myself to be dragged from my room and taken on a 'day trip'.

I realised what was happening as we got to the bridge. Cal had run on ahead and so when we came down to the riverside he greeted us, waving a pole and wearing a boater hat he'd managed to persuade one of the professional punters to give him.

He said (and by 'said' I mean 'shouted at an uncomfortable volume'), 'We're going to do as many touristy things as we can in one day. Starting with punting. Now, tell me that's not the most awesome idea ever!'

I was about to do as he said and tell him that it was not the most awesome idea ever, but Dan spoke first. I think *he guessed I would say something. He said, 'I would say it's oar-some,' and pointed at some oars on one of the rowing boats. 'Water good time we will have.'*

I looked at him and he said, 'Water – like "what a". Because we're going punting'. I replied that I had got it and that wasn't why I'd given him a look. Then he leaned in close and whispered, 'Be nice, or you're getting boat puns all day.'

Cal stood with one leg on the edge of the boat and one on the dock, helping each of us onto the boat. Except for Simon, who refused to take Cal's hand and then nearly fell off. When I got there Cal stopped me. He wanted to say thanks for helping him with the essays. And that even though he's gone and screwed it up anyway he was still grateful.

I said whatever, no worries and went to go past him, but he held out his hand. In it was something wrapped in a Sainsbury's bag.

He said he had got me a gift.

It was a chocolate cat.

Cal grinned and said it was 'Because I know how much you love Nigel.'

I looked down at the cat and then up at Cal. I saw Dan watching me from the boat.

So I thanked Cal and said I hoped that it all got sorted with him and Rosie.

I binned the cat later as soon as I got the chance, obviously, but the thought was nice.

I sat on the cushioned floor of the boat next to Dan. 'See

– I can be nice. So no boat puns,' I muttered to him. He whispered back, 'I shrimply wouldn't dare.'

Although he started a little overenthusiastically, Cal turned out to be quite good at punting. The others made half-hearted attempts, but as he seemed happy enough doing it we let him carry on. Needless to say I did not have a go. I'd ignored Dan's advice about wearing sensible shoes.

Cal gave a pretend tour, telling silly made-up stories about the buildings and scenery that we passed. At one point we pulled up alongside another boat, being punted by one of the official boathouse crew and he and Cal started trying to compete for an audience and shout the other down.

As Cal leaned over to shake the guy's hand and they slapped each other on the back, Dan let out a sigh. He turned to me and said, 'I hope he and Rosie sort things out soon. He's completely manic at the moment. When he sleeps in my room he keeps me up for hours chatting and trying to get me to play Xbox. Last night I ended up agreeing he could sleep in the bed with me because he kept mentioning how "uncomfortable and lonely" it is on the floor.'

I stifled a laugh and Dan turned to me with a confidential expression. He looked around and then said Cal had got on his nerves so much in bed that he had kicked him and pretended he was doing it in his sleep.

I told him I was shocked and appalled.

Dan grinned and said, 'Don't spread it around – everyone will want a piece if they find out I'm a bad boy'.

Later on, as we walked up from the boats into town,

the thing I'd been dreading happened.

Cal stopped in the middle of the pavement. He said that if we were being tourists for the day we had to go into one of the colleges. And how convenient – we were standing right next to one. I looked through the doorway and into the quad. I hadn't seen it in the daytime for a while. The dome was a glaring white in the sun, just like on that first day. I followed them up the steps slowly.

When I said it was my college they all turned back in surprise. Then Simon asked if that meant everyone could get in for free.

I nodded and told them I had a card – they could come in as my guests. I found it in my bag and walked to the front of the group. And then my heart stopped. Because someone with blond hair walked past one of the archways and for one mad, hopeful moment I thought . . . Well, it's obvious what I thought.

Dan was just behind me and quietly asked if I was okay. I nodded, still rooted to the spot. He frowned, then turned back to the others and said, 'Actually I want to go to Christ Church – the Harry Potter one.'

Simon asked if that would still be free.

I shrugged and said that my card worked in all of them, while tapping the card with my finger to hide the fact that my hands were shaking. I waited for them to decide.

Dan put his arm round my shoulder and said firmly that if not he'd pay for everyone. And that we could act out scenes from the films.

I shrugged his arm off and told him I'd rather stick pins

in my eyes, just as Cal shouted out, 'Shotgun Harry!'

Dan had his back to me as we left so he didn't see me mouth, 'Thank you.'

On the way to Christ Church Cal suddenly stopped in the middle of the pavement again and Arlo smacked right into the back of him. This time it was because he'd seen Rosie, sitting on her own in a café.

He didn't go in, probably because he didn't want to embarrass her, Dan said, after she'd pretended she was meeting a group of people. But I'd spotted something the rest of them hadn't – on the table in front of her were two cups. Looks like I'm not the only one lying . . .

Love you.

Cleo x

Chapter 26

When they get back I can hear laughing and shouting in the hall. The loudest voice is Cal's. I get a flash of anger then. He lied, too. Maybe if he hadn't done that I wouldn't have turned mental and started checking his phone.

And now I'm pacing around the room feeling like I can't go downstairs and be with everyone because of him.

I lean against the door and my chest is rising up and down as I try to control my breathing.

I'm making a fool out of myself being here.

The sound of his foot on the stairs strikes through everything. My heart leaps, but the rest of me is still pulsing with anger. My head feels all over the place. He reaches the landing and stops. I clench my fist to prevent myself from flinging open the door and seeing him. There's a creak of the floorboard. I hold my breath. I'm listening so intently I can hear the material of his shorts as he moves. In my mind I can see him reaching out towards the door.

I stare at the door handle and I swear it moves ever so slightly.

I breathe in. And I wait.

And then his footsteps disappear upstairs.

I sit heavily down on the bed and rub my eyes in frustration. This is ridiculous. I can't go through life in a permanent state of panic, too scared to ever do anything. I'm going to start getting what I want. Like Martin said at lunch, if you want something in life, you have to go out there and make it happen, not hide in a bedroom.

Obviously he just said the first bit, not the bedroom bit.

I need a plan of action.

I'll do what I always do when I'm flustered and I want to get my brain in order – write a list. I grab my diary and a pen out of my bag and find a spare page to write on.

Which bits of my life need sorting?

1. Sell lots at work. Maybe even get offered some kind of extra responsibility before the end of the programme.
2. Have an amazing social life, full of parties and energetic discussions about current affairs/philosophy.
3. Cal.

The first one I can make an attempt at, with all the techniques Martin told me about. I basically need to pretend I've already made the sale – like I have some software that guarantees success implanted in my brain.

And no soul?

No, don't overthink it.

The second should be doable as well if I keep meeting up with the people from the course. It turns out that my birthday is the day after Martin's. He's having a party at his college and he says I should come. Even the meal I have to go to at my parents' private members' club on results day is looking less bleak as Martin's parents are members too and he says he might be there that evening for a birthday meal.

And I don't really know much about current affairs or philosophy, but I could start reading the papers and research things. Most of the conversations that take place in the house are about food, or whether you'd rather have hooves for hands or the head of a cow, or whether Cal could get through the whole day using his feet instead of his hands (he couldn't).

They do make me laugh, though.

But the thing with the people from the course is that they hardly know me, so I can reinvent myself and not just be Cal's shy girlfriend, like I am around the housemates.

Number three – that's the difficult one.

Because what do I want to happen?

Chapter 27

I keep refreshing the screen. They went live at nine but the website's so overloaded it keeps crashing. I just need to know if I got in. Mum's collecting the actual results from school, but I'd rather know before I talk to her.

I look over at the sales scoreboard. 'Ian' now has a sale to his name.

We'll try to forget the fact that she was so old she could barely hear what I was saying and may have thought I was her granddaughter.

I'm saved from the crippling guilt and shame by my phone ringing.

Wait a minute.

My work phone is ringing ... The one that I use to call people all day and that I was assured shows up as a withheld number. Has someone managed to call it back?

Maybe it's the old woman? Or the man who said people like me are scum and that I'd be better off being a prostitute? I don't fancy talking to him again, really. Or anyone.

Then Bruiser's arm reaches across my desk and hits the answer key and I hear my headset connect.

'H–hello?' I say, bracing myself.

'Am I speaking to Rosie?' the person says in a very proper manner.

'Yes.'

'YES. I got through! ARGHHHHHH.'

The sound blasts into my ears and everyone at my table looks up.

'It's Gabi, bitch!'

'Yeah, I worked that out,' I laugh.

Then I see Clint on one of his rounds. He's frowning curiously at me.

'I got through by pretending to be a proper person!' she says. 'It was great. I told them I wanted to talk you about that accident I had. And that it had to be you because I'd heard you were really good at scamming money out of hospitals or whatever it is you do.'

'Um,' I say, eyeing Clint. 'Thank you, Mrs Morgan. We really value positive feedback.'

'No problem,' says Gabi, apparently not noticing that I just called her Mrs Morgan. 'So, we have your results!'

Clint has turned away.

'What? How?' I hiss into the phone.

'We got here before your mum,' says Gabi. 'Nish

distracted the admin lady and Mia grabbed them. They rejected my initial plan, though.'

'Right.'

'Which was me and Max pretending to be your parents.'

'Gabi?'

'I had a speech prepared about how you were our medical marvel mixed-race baby and everything.'

'Gabi!'

'And a wig.'

'You have my results?'

Clint is walking back over, accompanied by a woman I've never seen before but who looks important and a bit scary.

'Oh yeah!' says Gabi. 'Okay, so I'll tell you ours first. I got an A in events management and a B in English – isn't that mental? And an E in photography, but to be fair I never went or took any photos. Mia got Bs, but that's irrelevant because she's abandoning us. Nish got As, obviously, so she's in.'

'Did you know you could be entitled to thousands of pounds in unclaimed PPI?' I say in a tone that is supposed to say, 'That's awesome!'

There's the sound of an envelope ripping.

'You got . . . As in history and economics. And a B in business. You little boffin!'

'Now I just need to take some details,' I say dully and Clint nods approvingly at me.

I got into uni.

But I feel sort of empty. Relieved, initially, but after that, nothing.

Gabi's saying my name on the other end of the phone.

She thinks I've gone. And then she hangs up. I make a face at Clint that says, 'So close!' and he shakes his silly slicked-back head at me.

The event reminder on my phone pings. Dinner with parents in London. It's going to go off on Cal's phone, too. I added it to his calendar because he's so forgetful.

Today's also the day of his resit exam. If he does it.

Chapter 28

'We'll have some aperitifs before the meal, my good man.'

My dad hands his coat to the man on the desk and gives him a big grin. A bit like the one that his publicist told him to do at photo shoots and that I found him practising one day at home.

'You need to put your tie on, sir,' says the man as he turns and hangs up the coat.

Dad laughs as if rules like that couldn't possibly apply to him and strolls up the stairs to the bar entrance, where he's stopped by a woman who says he can't come in unless he adheres to the dress code.

He laughs and then makes a show of being told off as he fishes his ties out of his jacket pocket.

'They don't like a maverick, do they?' he says to me and Mum. I just smile like I usually do when he's being a bit embarrassing (and because the woman on the door is glaring). Mum is sending an email on her phone and ignores him.

He orders the drinks, ridiculously overpronouncing the name of the sherry, in complete contrast to how he was just talking to the taxi driver, calling him 'mate' and speaking with a slight cockney accent.

We sit in the lounge area and wait for our drinks. I look at my phone to see if my sister's texted. I don't have much hope for her getting past the door staff, considering that when I told her I thought they were fussy about shoes she said, 'Okay, so I have to wear shoes' like she was making a mental note.

Nothing from Poppy, but I do have a message from Martin.

`Nice dress x`

I scan the room and see them immediately, sitting around a table by the window. They are one of those families who all look alike. The dad has icy blue eyes, the same as Martin's, thin lips, a sharp face and a bald head. The woman has white blond hair tightly cropped around her face, which is angular and striking.

Martin says something to his parents and then the three of them walk over to our table.

Dad is delighted when Martin's mum immediately recognises him as Dave Hunter, MP. His actual name is Hugo, but he thinks taxi drivers will vote for him if he's called Dave.

They introduce themselves as Jeffrey and Lena Morton-Spitz and their son Martin, which Dad correctly guesses makes them the Morton-Spitzes of Morton-Spitz Sausages. He invites them to 'pull up some chairs and join the family' – well, me and him, as Mum has gone off to make a phone call.

Martin sits down next to me, just as his mum waves her hand at him and says, 'Oh yes, Martin's about to go into his second year at Oxford . . .' and then they launch into a comparison of their children, which Mum joins in with as she sits back down.

'If we're going to be talked about, perhaps we should talk about them?' Martin says to me out of the corner of his mouth. 'Dad is currently undertaking an alcohol addiction, while Mum's just got into a very inappropriate relationship with her PA, Colin.'

I laugh in surprise. 'Well, Dave Hunter's real name is Hugo.'

'Really?' he says, sounding amused. He has a dark blue suit on today and just like all the others it fits perfectly. And he always smells amazing. The other times we've met I've had to resist the urge to smell him. He's the sort of person my mum would call 'well turned out'.

As if she's somehow read my mind, Mum starts telling Martin's mum how smart her son is. He smiles politely.

I get a fluttery feeling in my chest seeing how much she likes him.

That's happened a few times now when I'm around Martin, though I've tried to ignore it.

'It's a far cry from green shoes,' says his dad with an odd smile.

Martin's mum pauses with her glass almost to her lips and blinks. Martin's expression hardens.

'Well,' says Mum, obviously not sure what to make of all this. 'Rosie, is your sister on her way?'

'Oh you have two, do you?' says Mrs Morton-Spitz as I tell Mum I don't know.

'Yes.' Dad nods. 'Poppy and Rose. Very . . . different girls.'

'Twins?' says Mr Morton-Spitz.

Mum shakes her head and then starts describing me and Poppy as if she's forgotten I'm sitting here.

The waiter comes over with a Pimms for me and a lemonade for Martin.

'No Pimms for you?' I say.

He shakes his head. 'I don't tend to drink.' Then he leans towards me and gives a slight smile. 'Doesn't mean I can't have fun.'

Ignore the fluttery feeling. Don't try to smell him.

My phone starts buzzing in my bag. It's Poppy. I look around to try and work out whether I'm allowed to answer it in here or not. Mum marched through the room on her phone, but I don't think anyone would dare tell her off. No one ever does. Whereas when people see me I think it's clear that the only danger is that I'll apologise too forcefully.

'You can use it on the stairs – I'll show you,' Martin says.

When we get there the phone's stopped ringing, but as I go to call her back it starts up again.

'Hey, what is it?'

'Ro, there's a problem.'

'Did you forget to wear shoes?'

There's a pause. She's actually checking.

'Nope, got shoes. I've also accidentally got your boyfriend.'

163

Chapter 29

Please don't let him be wearing his shorts.

Cal is patting the cloakroom attendant, who looks very uncomfortable, on the shoulder.

'Come on, dude. Who wears ties?'

'Our members, sir,' says the attendant in a tired voice.

Poppy walks in through the door and waves.

'Went for a smoke,' she says and indicates towards Cal. 'This has been going on for a while.'

Cal looks over to see who she's talking to and sees me. He grins lopsidedly and spreads his arms.

'I was invited, right?'

I nod. All I feel is panic, like I've been caught out. But at the same time my heart melts when I look at him standing there in a crumpled white shirt and black trousers. He looks like he's in school uniform.

'I can lend you a tie. I have a spare,' comes Martin's soft, low voice from behind me.

'Who's this guy?' laughs Cal and then he stumbles.

'Martin Morton-Spitz. A new friend,' says Martin, smiling pleasantly at him. 'Anyway, it must be nearly time to eat. We should all get to the dining room.'

He holds out a tie to Cal, which Cal takes, eyeing him warily.

'Since when are you friends with Draco Malfoy?' he mutters to me as we walk upstairs.

I'm about to ask him how the exam went when he strides ahead into the restaurant.

'Hey, guys!' He waves over at the table and immediately trips up on the carpet.

Well, this is going to be fun.

Our cutlery clinking is the only sound as everyone eats, staring awkwardly down at their plates. Everyone except Poppy, who never really notices stuff like this and is happily munching away. I steal a glance at Cal, who is sitting diagonally opposite me, but before I can get anything from him my mum interrupts.

'Callum,' she says, dabbing at nothing on her chin with her napkin. 'What have you been doing with your summer?'

Cal looks up and swallows food too quickly, almost choking.

'I work in this awesome pub. You guys should come down for a drink. It does great burgers!'

His voice is so loud. I scan the room to see if anyone is

looking at us and meet Martin's eye. The Morton-Spitzes are on a different table, but he is right in my eyeline.

'It's all work experience,' says Dad, like he's imparting great wisdom.

'As long as you move on at some point,' says Mum crisply and then she looks over at Poppy, who looks up with a mouth full of food.

'Huh?'

'Don't want to be working in a pub all our lives, do we?'

'Oh I got sacked from there,' says Poppy. 'I teach old people to dance now.'

'Cool!' says Cal and Mum and Dad give each other a look.

'Seriously,' says Cal to Poppy, stabbing a potato with his fork. 'You just do stuff and don't care what people think. I love it.'

He looks at me. I feel like I've been kicked in the chest.

'What's up with Steven?' Poppy whispers to me.

When Cal gets up, unsteadily, to go to the loo, Mum leans over to me.

'Is everything *usual* with you and him, Rosie?'

It's like someone asking if I'm okay. I don't trust my voice to answer without shaking.

'They had an argument,' Poppy chimes in. 'Nothing major.'

How does she know?

'What about?' Dad looks to me and then Poppy. He looks concerned and maybe a bit hurt. I think maybe he's offended I didn't mention anything during any of our phone calls.

166

He's always telling people how close we are. Poppy does her usual vague shrug. But I know it's a fake this time.

Mum and Dad share another look before Mum speaks again.

'You're very young, Rosie. Perhaps it might be an idea to, you know, cut your ties. You'll meet so many new people at uni.'

Dad looks like he might say something, but doesn't.

'It was just an argument,' I say quietly.

'Look, you know how ... fond we are of Callum,' Mum says delicately.

Dad nods. 'Very lively.'

'But you may find that as you get older you outgrow him a little. You're so bright and ambitious and Callum's ... well, rather on the laid-back side, isn't he?' I see her eyes flick over to the Morton-Spitzes' table. 'You might find that there are others who are more ... suited to you.'

'If that happens, it would be great if you could let me know.' Cal is standing by the table. He stays there, trying to look defiant, but I can see his eyes are shining. Cal's hardly ever sarcastic. Then a guest walks up to him and tries to order a bottle of wine. Cal looks down at his shirt, tie and black trousers.

'I'm not a waiter,' he says and sits back down.

No one says anything and Cal drains his wine glass.

'Listen, mate,' says Dad in his taxi-driver voice. 'Relationships aren't easy.'

Cal doesn't say anything.

Dad throws his hands up. 'We haven't made a toast!' He

167

fusses round the table making sure everyone has something in their glass. When he gets to Cal he deliberately gives him only a dribble.

'Rosie,' says Dad. 'A very happy birthday and congratulations on top-notch A-levels. And I'm quite sure you'll make a success of everything you do.'

Well, except for my relationships and the fact I'm the worst-performing person in the company at my job.

Mum clinks my glass. 'And we'll appeal on that B,' she says.

Thanks, Mum.

Cal has a smile plastered on his face. When our glasses clink our eyes meet. Cal frowns for a moment.

'I'd like to make a toast, too.'

Oh God.

'Oh dear,' says Mum under her breath.

Cal holds his now-empty glass above his head.

'What I want to say . . .' He's slurring his words and his arm sways to the side. 'Oh sorry.'

He'd bumped into the waiter, who was bringing out the puddings.

'Pannacotta – get in!' says Poppy.

I'm hoping Cal's been distracted.

'What I want to say,' he says even louder, 'is that, actually, "mate"' – he points at my dad – 'it *is* easy. I love you.'

'What?' says Dad.

'I love Rosie. I was looking at Rosie,' says Cal.

It was quite hard to tell as he's gone a bit cross-eyed.

I look down at my hands, wanting it all to stop.

'I love you!' he shouts and his voice echoes around the room. 'And I'm so sorry I lied, but it was only because I never feel good enough for you. But I love you and that's what matters, isn't it?'

I feel all the eyes on me. I just want him to shut up.

'Cal, stop it. Everyone's looking.'

'So?' he says and then turns to look round the room. 'Hello!' he waves. 'Don't mind me – just telling my girlfriend I love her. You go back to talking about money or bringing back slavery or whatever it is.'

'She said *stop*,' says Mum, her voice low and cold. Someone at another table is talking to a waiter and pointing in our direction. The waiter comes over.

'We've had a request that you either quiet down or leave, sir.'

Cal and the waiter look to the table.

'Probably best if you go, son,' says Dad.

Cal stands up. I can't meet his eye. And then I accidentally catch Martin's across the room and he gives me a sympathetic smile.

'Rosie.' Cal is watching us. He doesn't sound angry any more, just sad. He starts taking off the tie and it gets stuck, and he fiddles with it to try and undo the knot. Then he stops and looks at me.

'You wouldn't do this for me,' he says.

'Take your tie off?' I almost laugh at how random that seems.

'No, tell me you love me in front of loads of people and not care what anyone thinks.'

169

Oh.

He wrenches the tie free and throws it over to Martin, who picks it up off the floor. 'Thanks . . .' Martin says, his eyebrow raised. Then the waiter puts his hand firmly on Cal's shoulder and leads him away.

Ten minutes after he's gone I get a text from him.

`I dropped out, by the way.`

Chapter 30

'HAPPY BIRTHDAY EVE TO MY FAVOURITE SISTER!'

Poppy bats the side of my face with her hand until I open my eyes.

'Get up! We're going out for breakfast,' she says and I turn over, away from her. Then she pulls the duvet completely off me and onto her side of the bed.

I reluctantly sit up. 'Why can't we eat here?'

'The milk's gone hard,' she says, shoving me out of bed with her foot.

I look around the room. Poppy's flat is on the top floor of one of those big Victorian houses, which means her room is big, but it is also freezing, as there's no double glazing. And the wallpaper is peeling in places. And I spent a while earlier staring at some odd stains on the ceiling.

'That's because you don't have a rota for buying it,' I say and examine my face in the mirror. I don't really look like I'm on the brink of becoming a proper adult. More like an irritable person with mad hair.

'I didn't realise you were turning forty tomorrow.' She hunts for her bag. When she finds it she looks inside.

'Um, Ro?'

'I can pay for breakfast. My birthday present from Mum and Dad looks very much like it might be money.'

It's an envelope with *R – birthday money* written on it.

'Oh thanks, Ro.' Poppy takes off her pyjama top and looks around on the floor for her bra. 'I always get vouchers.' She frowns.

'That's because you'd spend it on something weird, whereas they know all I'll do is go crazy buying stationery or sensible shoes.'

'Do you think it's because of the time I bought a goat?' She chucks her pyjama trousers on the bed.

'Yes, I do.'

I grab what I hope are Poppy's keys off the side as she wanders out into the stairway leaving the door wide open. Then I suddenly panic as I am locking it that a neighbour will see me. Poppy told me that this place isn't a squat, but I think that one of her flatmates could have just told her that and she wouldn't question it. Also, it isn't very clean and no one appears to have a job.

Can you get in trouble for being the guest of a squatter?

But, as I follow my sister down the grimy concrete stairs, I think how much I'd rather be here in my sister's grotty London flat than at home with Mum and Dad going on about uni. Or in Oxford where I'd have to see Cal.

There's a café on the same road as Poppy's house, so we pull up some chairs and sit at an outside table. Poppy orders two of their 'best breakfasts' so I'm not entirely sure what we'll be eating.

'Thanks for having me,' I say and Poppy shrugs mid-cigarette.

'Any time. Do you need to stay tonight?'

'Oh no – I'm going back to Oxford.'

Poppy nods. 'You sorting things out with Cal then?'

I look up in surprise. Poppy asking a question relevant to the situation is very rare. And she got his name right.

'No – well, not really. Maybe. I'm, um, going for a drink with that guy from the other night,' I say quickly.

'Who was that?' she says suspiciously.

Well, this is a brilliant time for Poppy to turn into Miss Marple.

'Just that guy Mum and Dad were talking to. He's my mentor on the internship programme I'm doing. It's his birthday today so he's having a party and he said I should go and I don't have anything else to do, so I am.'

Am I talking too much? I shouldn't have to hide it. I can go for a drink with whoever I want. I can meet up with people I hardly know and be spontaneous and have a wild time.

I'm not so sure that I can really, but perhaps if I say it enough it will become true.

'Cool,' says Poppy. 'Oh, eggs. Brilliant!'

Chapter 31

I'm meeting Martin at the crossroads that leads down to his college at five-thirty. The party starts with drinks outside apparently, so he wanted to make sure it would still be warm enough. Is it a bit sad that my birthday-eve plans are tagging along to someone else's party?

All the way from the station I was panicking that I would see Cal or one of the other housemates. Then when I was waiting at the crossroads (early as usual) I saw someone who looked a bit like Simon, had a mini heart attack and ran down the High Street. Then I saw someone who looked like Dan coming the other way and I dived into the nearest shop. Which turned out to be one of those shops that sell the ceremonial robes and those gowns Oxford students wear (and always reminded me of something from Diagon Alley). I didn't want to admit I hadn't meant to go in there so I ended up saying I wanted to buy a robe. The man asked if I was matriculating in September and I said no, I just liked the robes. He told me to come back on Monday as he was about to close, which is code for 'Please leave, you weirdo.' I don't even think it was Simon and Dan anyway.

The street now seems clear of housemate doppelgängers, so I walk back up the road. My heel catches on a gap in the pavement, my ankle gives way and I nearly go flying. I'm not doing a very good job of sneaking through town.

I did think of telling Cal I was here. Then I could stay in the house. But Martin said he could arrange for me to stay in one of the rooms in college if I wanted. And I haven't heard from Cal since I replied to his dropping-out text to say I hoped he was okay.

I stumble again on another pavement crack. It's because I hardly ever wear heels. I'm taller than Gabi and Mia when they are in them anyway. Nish isn't bothered about towering over all of us with her long legs, but I don't like to stick out. And everyone is small next to Cal.

But Martin said there was a smart dress code. So I borrowed these shoes from Poppy and then we went shopping for a new dress. It was like being kids again. When I was nine and Poppy turned thirteen she was allowed to take me into town. (Although Mum did ask me to make sure Poppy didn't do anything silly, so I'm not sure who was taking who really.) We'd spend all morning trying on different outfits and then get milkshakes. I hadn't realised how much I miss hanging out with Poppy since she left home. Today we tried on loads of dresses and argued just like old times. I couldn't zip up one of her dresses and she blamed my 'fat hands'. I didn't say that the dress was at least two sizes too small. Not that Poppy would care – she'll squeeze herself into a tight dress and flaunt her curves without being at all self-conscious. Whereas I try to hide my lack of curves in shift dresses. Poppy persuaded me to try this dress on. It's much more on the figure-hugging side than I am really comfortable with. And it has gypsy sleeves, so it's more low-cut then my usual style too. I tried to argue that I have no boobs, but Poppy just shrugged and said, 'So?'

For a moment I really wish I was still with her. We could have stayed at hers and watched films. She said she didn't have any plans tonight and it was a shame I have to go to this thing.

Only I don't have to go, do I? But here I am. Or I could have invited her. But I didn't. I tap on my handbag uneasily as a guilty thought strikes. It's because I would be embarrassed introducing her to the people from the course. It was like Cal said – she does what she wants and doesn't care what people think. So does he. But I can't seem to not care what people think.

I'm rescued from the soul-searching by Martin arriving with a group of people in suits and nice dresses, chatting and laughing loudly.

This was a mistake. I shouldn't have tried to be spontaneous; I should have stayed at home in the possible squat where the only danger was accidentally drinking hard milk.

'Good evening,' he says, one eyebrow raised.

He is a bit like Draco Malfoy, actually. There's something slightly sly about him. He'd definitely be in Slytherin, anyway. I'm not sure what to make of that since, according to my friends, I am one hundred per cent Hufflepuff.

'Hello!' I say. 'Happy birthday.' I smile at him and then wave at the others behind him. Some of them are from the course, but most I don't know.

'Just to warn you,' I say as we start down St Aldate's. 'If there is a "getting served alcohol" issue, I can't lie in those situations. I'll just run.'

'So we need to keep you hidden until midnight?' he says. 'Shame, when you look so lovely.'

I don't really know what to say to that. And my mind immediately flicks to a memory of Cal and when I was doing one of my mad early-morning revision sessions and I woke up at four in the morning and couldn't sleep. I hadn't realised he'd woken up too and was looking over at me. I was in pyjamas with all my hair piled on top of my head and frowning through my glasses at the piles of notes. He said, 'You look lovely.' I said, 'I really don't.' He said, 'I love you.'

'So I'll just be on the Diet Cokes till then,' I say to fill the huge, awkward silence that followed his comment.

'No problem.' He smiles at me.

I've had more than my usual two drinks. Now is definitely the time to stop. When the first Diet Coke arrived I took a sip. It was Diet Coke and whisky. Martin caught my eye from across the quad and winked.

I smiled back and held the glass in the air, but I felt a

177

twinge of annoyance. I know he probably thought he was helping me get past the age problem, but I didn't ask him to.

I managed to make the drink last for the rest of the outside bit (mainly because it tasted really strong and quite horrible), before we were led in to dinner. We were at one end of one of the tables in the Great Hall, which is as grand as it sounds – all wooden panelling and the walls lined with portraits. There was wine already out on the table and through the meal Martin kept pushing my glass towards me. I noticed he was doing it to other people too, but they didn't seem to mind. When he got up to go and speak to a waiter at the other end of the room I heard a ginger guy whispering to the girl with long brown hair next to him.

'Martin's, like, so full-on today, isn't he?'

The girl rolled her eyes at him. 'Well, *yeah* . . .' she said, but she didn't get the chance to finish, because Martin came back over.

'It's absinthe,' says a guy with dark, wavy hair.

We are in an upstairs room somewhere in the college. I must have been staring at this guy without realising. I did vaguely wonder what he was up to, pouring water over sugar into a glass of something green, but mainly I was wondering if Cal is going to wish me happy birthday. I've just been sitting on the sofa hardly talking to anyone. And thinking about all of the people I could have been spending my birthday with. The guy hands the glass to me.

'Have you never tried it before?' he says.

'Oh no, I've had it loads of times. Yum!' I take a sip.

It is in fact the most disgusting thing I have ever tasted.

'Mmm. I'm just going to . . . tell lots of other people how nice this is.'

I creep off to the toilets, planning to throw it away and get a normal drink.

I walk straight into Martin. He puts both hands on my shoulders and smiles at me, his eyes sparkling. I remember his friends' conversation from earlier about him being full-on and I'm suddenly struck by the thought of how little I really know about him.

'Having fun?'

'Yep!'

'Good,' he says softly and grins at me. Then he says, 'What?' and I realise I've been frowning at him.

'Oh, nothing. I was just going . . .' I point to the other side of the room, where I assume the toilets are.

I'm not used to not knowing what is going on behind someone's eyes. I always thought Cal was an open book. If he smiles it's because he's happy (usually due to something food-related) and if he looks sad it's because he's sad. Like when he left the meal.

I walk quickly past Martin, hoping there won't be a queue for the toilet because I think I'm about to cry.

I lock the door and lean against it. And I finally let all the sad things I've been thinking show on my face.

And Cal will never know because I'm crying in silence in a place full of strangers.

Last autumn was the first time I visited him in Oxford and

he picked me up and spun me round as soon as I came through the ticket barriers, making me drop all my bags and annoying all the other people who'd just got off the train. I hit him on the shoulder to make him put me down.

Walking along the platform, holding his hand, I was making a list in my head of things to worry about.

1. I realised on the train I missed a bit when I was shaving my legs. I may have to angle my leg away from him the whole weekend.

2. I think my hand is turning clammy holding his. Maybe I should mention it in case he thinks I've got clammy skin all over.

3. What if his housemates make a group decision that they don't like me and ask me to leave?

4. What if when Cal said we could have a long-distance relationship he was just being polite and he's leading me off to dump me?

5. It would be nice if I could stop spending all my time in my head and just enjoy something.

I'd only been going out with him for about two months, and that had been the summer holidays, when we were in the same town with all our friends around us. I'd started to relax around him and begin to be more myself, when the summer ended. He was going back to his uni life, which didn't include me at all. What if I didn't fit in to it?

We got into his house and only Arlo was in the front room, so I was introduced to him and was slightly relieved to meet someone else who was socially awkward.

As he closed the door to his room Cal narrowed his eyes at me.

'What's up?' he said.

'Nothing, I'm fine! We should probably start getting ready for dinner.'

'It's three-thirty.'

He tried to peer at me and I turned away. So he went over to the bed and lay down with his arms folded.

'I've got all night.'

'You haven't,' I said. 'We're going out for dinner.'

He shrugged. 'You may as well tell me now because I can be really annoying when I want to be.'

I gave him a look and he patted the bed next to him. I walked over and sat down, then I looked at him and his smile made me smile too. And I thought that I could tell him what I was thinking and it would be okay.

While I was thinking that he shoved his knee in my back.

'What's up?'

And he kneed me again.

'Give me a chance!' I shouted. And he did it again.

'STOP IT!'

Cal gave a huge laugh.

'I knew your mean side would come out sooner or later.'

He made me smile again.

'Okay,' I said. 'I'll tell you. But you're going to end up thinking I'm a nutcase.'

'I can deal with that. Everyone's a bit nutty really.'

So I told him all the things I worried about. About how I spent all my time in my head. And I was afraid of letting myself enjoy being with him, or admit how much I liked him, in case it all went wrong.

I didn't mention the hairy leg and the clammy hand. Some worries should remain secret.

He listened, just letting me talk, and when I'd finished he looked up at me with a thoughtful expression. When he spoke his voice was lower and quieter than usual.

'You know, it's a relief to hear that you're scared, because I'm bloody terrified.'

'Really? You don't seem like you'd ever be scared.'

'Yeah! I'm scared you're going to turn round at some point and realise you're going out with a complete idiot! I didn't care about anything before I met you. Now there's something that matters to me.'

We never went to the restaurant.

I look at my face in the mirror. I look a mess. I dab at the mascara so I don't have to go back in there with panda eyes. I pause for a moment. And then I call him.

Chapter 32

'Where have you been?' says Martin. He's leaning on a wall by the door and puts his hand out to stop me as I pass.

'Just mingling.'

In the toilet. On my own.

'You've finished your drink.' He taps the empty glass.

If by 'finished' you mean 'tipped down the sink', then yes I have.

'We can't have you empty handed.'

'I'm fine, thanks – I don't really feel like another.'

Despite what I've said, Martin appears a few minutes later with another drink. He smiles at me and says that as I'm the 'birthday girl' I should be having a good time.

And I should be. I should be having fun and forgetting I care about anything. Just like Cal is right now, from the sounds of it.

Before I can reply, Martin's gone again. I watch him, walking up to different groups, throwing lines into their conversations. Up until now I've been sort of in awe of his confidence – how smooth he is and how he always seems to say the right thing. But now it's annoying. And patronising. He puts down drink after drink on the table. And I manage to dispose of each one without him noticing. Sometimes giving them away, sometimes running off to the loo.

I'm doing a good job of convincing him I'm having a good time, although he may think I have cystitis.

I look around the room and it lurches slightly. The drinks from before are definitely more than enough.

The guy with dark, wavy hair holds out his hand.

'Hi, I'm Peter. But my friends call me Paedo.'

I'm not entirely sure what to say to that. *How nice, I'm Rosie, but my friends call me Sex Offender?*

'As bants,' he adds.

Oh, well, that's okay then.

I'm all ready to come up with some excuse and quietly go to the room I'm staying in. Martin pointed it out earlier, so I should be able to find it. But then I remember what I heard when Cal answered the phone. He's not moping around, crying in toilets and going to bed early. He's out with a load of laughing girls.

Two can play at that game.

Maybe.

I tell 'Paedo' I'm just going to make a quick phone call and duck out of the door, which leads to the top of a winding staircase. I take out my phone and go on Facebook. Just a quick status about who I'm out celebrating my birthday with and what an amazing time I'm having. So he knows I'm not a loser who can't have fun without him.

Then I see it.

He's changed his profile picture. It's not the one of him with his arms round me while he's biting my ear. It's him standing on a boat and brandishing a punting pole. The cover photo isn't the Will and Lyra bench any more, it's them all on the punt. Everyone in the house except me. And his relationship status has disappeared.

I feel hollow. Two days ago he was telling a restaurant full of people he loved me. Now he's publicly moving on.

'Paedo' is sitting by one of the windows that look back down over the quad. I wave at him, take a deep breath, go over and sit on the sill next to him and start talking. It turns out it is actually quite easy to talk when everything you say is the opposite of what you mean.

'The placement – it's just so . . . me, you know? I thrive on the rush of clinching a sale.'

I dread going in every morning and when I did sell some insulation to an old lady I went and hid in the toilets for ten minutes because I felt so guilty.

'Absinthe is like, okay – I mean, I'll drink it if it's there, but it's by no means my favourite of the spirits. When I'm out socialising I prefer a G & T.'

I want some Ribena.

'I'm actually glad we broke up. Now I can do what I want and come to things like this, which is *so much fun.*'

I have no idea what I mean. Or think. Or feel.

Peter Paedo looks interested in what I'm saying and nods in all the right places. He's not bad-looking, even though he is slurring his words and says 'bants' a lot.

After a few more minutes of inane conversation he leans in close and his fringe flops over his eyes.

'You know, Ruby, I'd really like to kiss you.'

I could say 'Oh no thanks' or 'It's getting late' or 'That's not my name', but, because I'm me, I say, 'Ooh, go on then!'

Go on then? That will be a lovely story to tell our grandchildren. Who will know me as Grandma Ruby.

It's not the most amazing kiss. A bit like those first kisses at school discos when you are just working out that mouths are for kissing as well as eating and there is a bit of overlap in the technique.

His tongue is squirming around in my mouth like a slug. Not that I'm much better, I'm sure, seeing as my head is spinning and my mind is somewhere else. At one point I actually forget to keep moving my mouth. I can hear people commenting in the room and a few voices calling out from down in the quad.

I feel sick.

'What's the time?' I say suddenly. Into his mouth.

'Huh?' he says, into mine.

I pull my face away from him. 'What's the time?' I repeat, but I don't give him a chance to answer. I pick up my bag and move away from the window and out of his reach. I don't know what I was thinking.

I take my phone out and press the menu button. The photo of me and Cal appears. The same one that he's just taken off his Facebook profile. The time is displayed across our faces. Midnight.

I'm eighteen.

And I'm with a whole load of people I don't know.

Soon my phone starts buzzing as Mia, Gabi and Nish all message me. Mia sends a picture of a sloth with its thumbs up. Nish sends one of four old ladies on a night out with a message saying, The one with her skirt tucked into her knickers is you. Happy b'day dude x

Gabi's is all capital letters and exclamation marks and her saying how she has the celebration weekend all planned and she thinks I'm going to love it.

I need to leave.

I say a general goodbye, but I don't think anyone really notices. When I look back at Peter he's already chatting to another girl, so I don't think he'll be too heartbroken.

When I walk out of the door someone is sitting on the top step of the winding staircase.

Martin twists round and looks at me. His face is flushed and his eyes are bloodshot. Then I see he's holding a bottle of whisky.

'I thought you didn't drink?'

'Well, it's my birthday, isn't it?' he says in a low voice. He lifts up the bottle, does an imaginary cheers and smiles, but no part of his face looks happy.

'Are you okay?' I say, slightly unnerved. He seems so

different to his usual confident, controlled self. And he's blocking my way down the stairs.

'Fine,' he snaps and takes a swig from the bottle.

'Okay, well I'm going to head to bed now.'

'I thought you were having a good time.' He's looking at me and frowning. And he still hasn't moved from the stairs.

'I was – I did. But I'm going, so if you could . . .'

To my relief he stands up. But as I go on to the first step he suddenly puts his hand on the bannister, trapping me.

'Come on, don't be boring. Life's too short!'

He has tears in his eyes.

I duck under his arm and move a few steps down, my heart thumping.

'Look, I don't know what's going on, but I am going. I think maybe you should go to bed too.'

Then I see his expression. His face is pale white and twisted in pure hatred. He's looking at me, I think, and then I realise he's looking down the stairs behind me. His eyes look like they're on fire.

'What's she doing here?'

I turn to look, but as I do I get the familiar racing heart and sudden cold feeling. The whole staircase swims in front of my eyes and then it all goes black.

Chapter 33

'Cal was worried after you called. So he phoned your sister to find out when/if you were coming back. She told him you'd gone out with someone called Spitty Marvin. I talked to her and worked out who she meant. He's bad news, so I told Cal I'd come down and find you.'

Cleo is sitting on her windowsill and I'm on her bed with my hands wrapped around a big mug of tea. Nigel the cat is kneading Cleo's leg, but she doesn't appear to mind.

'So who was the dude you were kissing in the window?' she says.

'You saw?'

She nods. ''Fraid so.'

'Oh God.' I put my head in my hands. 'He said his name was Peter, but his friends call him Paedo. As banter,' I say miserably.

Cleo bursts out laughing. I look at her and can't help laughing too. I turn a bit hysterical and I can't stop.

'I don't know if I'm laughing or crying!' I say.

There's a short silence and Cleo scratches Nigel's chin. I slept in here last night after she rescued me. I've thanked her about twelve times, until she told me it was annoying. But seeing as she caught me just as I fainted and stopped me falling down a flight of stairs I thought twelve thank yous was fair.

'How did we get home?' I say as it occurs to me that I have no memory of it.

'With difficulty,' she says. 'You'd gone delirious so I shoved you in a taxi.'

'I remember someone carrying me.'

Cleo flexes her muscles.

'You seemed to want to take me to your sister's – you said I needed to find a squat next to a café.'

'Oh God, I'm so sorry.'

She shrugs. 'It's fine. At first I thought you were telling me to squat next to a café, which was more weird.'

'So how do you know Martin?' I say.

Cleo stiffens. 'He . . . uh, we used to hang out last term. I was good friends with his sister, but we kind of all fell out.'

'Oh, I'm sorry,' I say.

Cleo doesn't reply. She's frowning and concentrating on stroking Nigel. She looks like she might be trying not to cry.

'Let's talk about something else,' she says. 'So, you're eighteen.'

'And I celebrated by throwing myself down the stairs.'

She laughs. 'There's a gift for you somewhere. We had to go on a "house shopping trip" to buy it.'

I don't ask if that was Cal's idea. In case she says no. Instead I say, 'Well, you've had the day out, the movie night and the shopping trip. That makes you a fully initiated housemate.'

She rolls her eyes but has a slight smile. 'They've worn me down. I guess it's not so bad, having friends. I've even got used to the stupid cat. Had to, really – it never leaves my room except to shit.'

I think for a moment. About all the times I've been sitting with my friends and laughing so hard I couldn't breathe. And the hours of phone calls and messaging sessions and crisis coffees. That's what matters, isn't it? You can keep trying to get the Life part right, but the main thing is you have people to share it with. And that's what Cal was too. Someone to share things with. And laugh about them with. To be happy for you when things are good and there for you when they're not. It's like everything is suddenly in sharp focus. I slam my fist on the bed and say, 'I know what I've got to do!'

Tea sloshes over the side of my cup and onto Cleo's duvet and I apologise.

'Well, spit it out,' she says.

I take a deep breath. 'I'm not going to sit here being miserable about things not being how I want them. I'm going to go out and change them.'

'Sounds good,' says Cleo. 'What are you going to do?'

'Well . . .' I say. I don't want to lose the momentum. I'm

sort of making this up as I go along, but at the same time feel like I'm finally saying something I've been thinking the whole time.

'I'm going to make them take me off the phones on the internship,' I say firmly. 'And I'm going to phone up uni and tell them I want to do something else.'

'Wow, a girl with a plan,' says Cleo in her usual dry way, but she's smiling.

'Because if it still all goes wrong, it doesn't matter,' I carry on. 'Because I have awesome friends I can moan and laugh about it with.'

Cleo nods. 'Sounds like you do.'

'And do you know what else?' I hit the bed again with my hand.

'You're going to ruin my expensive duvet with tea?'

'Cal and I need a crisis coffee.'

Chapter 34

'My name's Patience and I'm calling to talk to you about that accident you had.'

I always forget that Bruiser's name isn't actually Bruiser.

I marched straight over to Clint's office when I arrived this morning. Well, I walked quickly up to the door, went to knock, decided he was probably busy and I should come back later and then he opened it anyway.

'I have something to say and I want you to listen —' I mumbled quietly.

'Rosie,' he interrupted. It is possible he didn't actually hear me. 'You're disappointing.'

'Oh,' I said. 'Sorry.'

'Four weeks and one hit. You know what it is? You're a nice person. And that's great if we're – I dunno – eating biscuits and talking about the weather, but this is business.

I need you to be a dick, but in a good way. Do you see what I'm saying?'

'Yes?' I wonder if I could get a job eating biscuits and talking about the weather?

'You don't have what it takes, Rosie.'

'Oh . . . dear.'

'For the last week of the placement I'm demoting you to making tea and doing data entry. And I'm cutting your pay. What do you say to that?'

'Thanks, Clint!'

He walked past, looking back in confusion at how happy I sounded.

I put Bruiser's tea down on the desk and she gives me a thumbs-up, before bringing her fist crashing down on the table and shouting, 'YES you can ignore the THOUSANDS of pounds of unclaimed money, but it's your children who will SUFFER when you can't afford to buy them birthday presents.' There's a brief pause while the person on the phone says something and then she adds, 'Or FOOD.'

I practically skip over to the next table. Being the tea lady means everyone is pleased to see me. I give Ron his tea with a supportive eye roll after Clint has just walked past and said, 'Keep it up, ladies.' Georgie and Tina are mid-rant when I get to them, so I agree with them for ten minutes that it is outrageous that Clint has reported them for talking when they are supposed to be working. Deborah beckons me closer when I deliver her tea and informs me that Toby in HR has a drinking problem and Piers in Accounts has a face like a ham. I don't know who either of those people are, but

I nod. And I work out which one Piers is anyway when I take tea to Accounts later.

And it gives me time to think. About the end of the summer. How everyone's nervous about it, but also excited. And I'm dreading it. Actually dreading it. And it's not because I always dread things and I should just be brave and face up to it. It's because this path isn't right. And for the right path I could be brave. And for the right person.

I get a bit carried away with my imaginary bravery and walk the tea trolley into a pillar. But I think I'm a bit closer to working out what I need to do. Or at least the next step. After I've mopped up the tea trolley and the floor.

Rosie has joined the conversation.

Rosie: I need to talk to you!
Rosie: Cal and I had a huge argument after I accused him of cheating on me, but it turned out he was actually going to be kicked off his course and he didn't want me to know.
Rosie: Then he turned up at my birthday meal drunk and said he loved me but I just sat there like a heartless lemon.
Rosie: Then I went out and kissed someone called Paedo.
Rosie: And fainted down some stairs.
Rosie: But now I want him back.
Rosie: (Cal, not Paedo.)
Rosie: I also want to drop out of my course and do something else but I don't know what!
Gabi: OMG x 6!!!
Mia: Well this is a lot to take in!
Nish: This is Nish's mother I do not know how to stop these messages.
Nish: I hope you are well Rosie.
Gabi: You sent it to Nish's old number you tit!
Gabi: I mean 'you fool'. Hello Mrs Lakhani! Just tap on the list of names at the top and select to leave the conversation.
Nish: Thank you Gabi goodbye girls.

Nish has left the conversation.

Mia: Brilliant.

Mia: Anyway, WHAT?! Are you okay?

Gabi: You should have told us! We would have come to Ox to cheer you up!

Rosie: I know. But sometimes it's hard to admit when everything's gone wrong. But I'm going to talk to him after work and tell him that I love him and that's what matters, not the course he does.

Mia: That's awesome ☺ Let us know how it goes.

Gabi: I'm gonna weep!! It's like something in a film!! Apart from the kissing Pervert bit.

Mia: Yeah maybe don't mention that in your heartfelt speech.

Rosie: I don't know – I think I should just tell him everything. There's been too much hiding things recently.

Mia: Okay, but don't open with it.

Gabi: ARGH I'm so excited. I didn't even know you'd broken up and now there's going to be an EMOTIONAL REUNION.

Rosie: Thanks guys! I'll let you know how it goes.

Mia: So what kind of course do you think you want to do then?

Rosie: I don't know. All I've got so far is something that involves working with people. Which I know is most jobs. But something where I was helping them would be nice.

Mia: You're good with kids.

Rosie: Am I??

Gabi: Yeah, when I tried to read a story to Max and Cal's evil little cousins they said 'The pretty curly girl does it better'.

Rosie: They're not evil – they're just a bit spoiled!

Gabi: George bit my leg and growled, but whatever. Anyway, children – yes!

Mia: A job taming evil children?

Nish has joined the conversation.

Nish: My mother says you've had some sort of breakdown.

Mia: Not a breakdown – a break-up, but it's all going to be okay!

Gabi: We're helping!

Rosie: ☺

Chapter 35

I have a couple of hours' data entry and then it's time to go home. I also get Nish to assure me that her mum won't tell my parents about me changing my course. Our parents aren't friends or anything, but in my head all mums are in a secret network where stuff like this is instantly broadcast to the group.

I wave goodbye to people on my way out and get some weird looks. They're probably wondering why I'm so cheerful. Or who I am. But it doesn't dampen my mood. The internship is suddenly quite fun. I might be getting somewhere on sorting out the course. Now for the relationship.

When I woke up in Cleo's room yesterday Cal had already gone out to work. Apparently he'd taken the double shift last minute because he didn't think I'd be celebrating my birthday in Oxford after what happened at the meal.

Neither did I, to be honest. The day ended up being really nice, because the housemates took me out for a picnic. I texted Cal a few times, but I was asleep when he got in from work and then he was asleep when I left this morning, so we haven't had the chance to talk properly. But I know he's free tonight. Dan said that when he spoke to him, Cal had no plans this evening except 'lying on the sofa in the nude'.

I redo my make-up in the work loos. I'm wearing the dress I wore on our first date. I get some food from the supermarket and text Dan asking if I could take over the kitchen this evening and possibly borrow some candles.

```
Wow, Rosie, you really know how to get on
my wick . . . Jokes! Of course you can
have the kitchen. Hope you guys have fun
☺
```

And all the way home I'm practising my speech. I'm so flustered thinking about it that I almost don't notice the envelope lying on the kitchen table.

Hey Rosie,

I've realised we just aren't going to sort this out. We're too different. You're going places and you don't want some drop-out who hasn't a clue what he's doing with his life dragging you down.

I'm going home for a few days to hang with my brother – think I need time to get my head straight and figure out what I want.

I've had an awesome year with you. You changed my life. Thank you for everything you've done and I'm sorry I couldn't be the guy who deserves you.

I hope we can be friends.

Love you always, Bumhead.

Cal x

Chapter 36

'So, guys,' says Clint. 'Even though it eats into our selling time, and so, into the profit the company makes, and so, ultimately into all of your wages, company policy requires us to have leaving nibbles and drinks for every departing employee, even temps.'

He lifts his small plastic cup and tilts his head at me.

'So I've provided nuts, because you can eat them quickly and, ideally, at your desks. And —'

His assistant Mary leans over and whispers in his ear.

'Except for Sue,' he carries on, 'who has a severe allergy. Sue, you should probably just leave the room because I have put the nuts everywhere.'

There's a pause as Sue leaves.

'You will also find bottles of fizzy grape juice, so as not to tempt any of you recovering alcoholics. So no slipping gin in it under your desk, Toby! Ha ha.'

Toby doesn't laugh.

'So everyone charge your cups and raise a toast to the temp,' says Clint.

'To Ian!' calls Ron and he points at my chart on the wall, with its one hit.

'To Ian!' shouts everyone else. And then we all go back to our desks to eat our individual portions of nuts.

So that's that. They end of my placement.

Simon and Arlo are both on their laptops and Dan is reading, while I wait downstairs in the living room for Cleo to get ready. We're going out for a drink. It's funny that she's the one I've turned to now. I've spent most of the evenings of my last week in her room. She worked out quite early on that I didn't really want to talk about Cal, so she didn't ask me. We've been discussing my changing courses plan and have come up with something I'm actually excited about (along with the usual nerves of course). But rather than just scary it feels like a challenge. And something I could do.

It's been a relief to talk about other stuff. It's not that I'm not grateful for all the texts the other girls have been sending me and for all the lovely things they're saying; it's just that it's a reminder of something I wish wasn't true. And every reminder is like reliving the moment I found out.

Just then I get a message from Gabi about how she's planned all these things to cheer me up at the party weekend and that boys are rubbish anyway. The pain goes sharp again. I sit there and wait for it to go back to just the dull, hollow ache and I realise Dan is looking at me.

'Is Cleo okay?' He frowns.

She has been in a bit of an odd mood since the night with Martin and the fainting. But I know she doesn't want to talk about it so, like she does with Cal, I haven't brought it up.

'Yeah, she's fine I think!' I say.

Dan narrows his eyes at me. He is about to speak when suddenly there's a deafening, screeching noise from outside, followed by a thud and a strange cry.

We all look at each other. No one wants to be the one that goes outside.

Eventually Dan moves towards the door, but as he does a figure appears at the glass and the doorbell rings, making him jump.

He opens the door to reveal a middle-aged man in glasses who looks pale and shaken.

'Did you have a pet cat?'

Chapter 37

When Dan comes back in with Nigel wrapped in a coat, Cleo is standing at the bottom of the stairs. I don't know how long she's been there. Her face is expressionless. Slowly she turns round and then she walks back up. We hear the door of her room shut.

'She never liked Nigel,' mutters Arlo.

We go back into the sitting room and Simon and I sink down into the sofa. Dan lays the bundle on the coffee table and sits on the arm of the chair, while Arlo hovers sadly by the window as if he's hoping there's been some mistake and Nigel is going to come running over and paw at the glass to be let in.

'We should have a proper funeral,' says Arlo, his voice choked up, and Simon nods in agreement.

I meet Dan's eye. We both know that we're the ones who

will go along with everything to keep the others happy and that neither of us will point out that burying a cat in the garden might go against the tenancy agreement.

'We should set her alight on a boat on the river,' says Simon.

'No we shouldn't,' says Dan.

'And someone needs to tell Cal,' says Arlo.

They all instinctively look at me, remember, and then look away awkwardly. Dan says that he'll give him a call. Then he says he'd better go and check if Cleo's okay as well. Arlo comments, 'Don't bother – it's not as if she cares,' but Dan ignores him and goes upstairs.

Arlo follows him out and starts throwing things around in the cupboard under the stairs. I assume he's looking for a coffin. Simon and I stand in the hallway watching him.

'She was such a good cat,' Arlo says as he throws a shoe and a tennis racquet out of the cupboard. 'Remember how she used to go round lapping up all the milk in the cereal bowls after breakfast so there wasn't as much washing up to do?'

I can't share as many Nigel memories, obviously. On one of the first nights I spent here I woke up and she was sitting on the pillow, about a centimetre away from my face, and I screamed. Cal said it was her way of welcoming me.

I mainly feel sad for them. Cal was always sending me pictures of him holding Nigel wearing some hat he'd made, or sending me videos of when he made her walk on her hind legs. If Nigel was anything, she was tolerant.

'You're never alone when you have a cat,' says Simon suddenly.

Arlo and I raise our heads in astonishment, but we don't have time to say anything because Dan comes back down the stairs.

'Cleo's gone.'

Dear M,
Everything I care about turns to shit.

Chapter 38

The window in Cleo's room is wide open and the curtains are billowing in the breeze.

'Maybe she jumped,' says Arlo.

'Or climbed down,' I say.

Simon and Dan lean out of the window and look down onto the empty patio.

'Maybe she fell and the body disappeared,' says Simon.

'Or she climbed,' I say.

Dan turns to Simon. 'She's not Sherlock!'

'Well, that doesn't make sense,' says Arlo. 'Because Sherlock didn't . . .' He sees the look we are collectively giving him. 'Okay, I'll go and see if she's anywhere else in the house.'

Arlo and Simon crash noisily down the stairs and a draught from the window sweeps through the room and I notice for the first time that there is a pile of paper in the middle of the room that is gradually being scattered.

I pick one up.

Dear M . . .

Dan starts picking them up.

'Who's M? Her mum?' he says.

I'm halfway through reading one of them.

'Um, I don't think so. Unless they have a really odd relationship.'

'Isn't it more likely it's a diary?' says Dan. 'I mean, she hasn't posted any of them.'

Then his cheeks go red. I saw his name on quite a few of the pages.

I can't make sense of any of this. I think 'M' must be Martin, but then why would she be writing letters saying she loves him?

'There was this guy,' I say slowly and Dan looks up at me. 'I know him, sort of, and I was with him on my birthday when Cleo came to find me. He looked really angry when he saw her. And she says he's bad news.'

Dan and I stand there, frowning as we look through the letters. None of this makes sense.

I decide to have a quick look on Martin's Facebook to see if there's any clue as to where he is.

There's a cry from the front of the house. So we go out of Cleo's room and into Cal's, which overlooks the road.

Arlo is standing on the pavement. 'My bloody car's gone!'

'How would she have got the key?' says Dan, when we go down and stand in the porch.

'I kept it under a plant pot in the front garden,' says Arlo.

Dan looks at him. 'Why?'

'So I didn't lose it in my room,' says Arlo.

'Why didn't you tell me that?'

'Why would I?' says Arlo.

'So I could tell you it was a stupid idea,' says Dan through gritted teeth.

'I knew,' says Simon.

'Yeah, me too,' I say quietly.

Dan gives an exasperated sigh and goes and sits on the stairs.

'We could get a taxi and go out looking for her?' I suggest.

'And tell it to go where?' Dan snaps.

He's usually the one calming everyone down, so it's even more unnerving when Dan is wound up.

'I knew I should have put that tracking device on her phone,' mutters Simon.

'Oh my God,' I say.

'Hey, calm down – I didn't!' frowns Simon.

'No,' I say, looking at the phone in my hand. 'His sister died.'

Everyone in the room turns to look at me and waits for me to make sense.

'That guy, Martin,' I say to Dan. 'There's a link to her tribute page on his wall. Because Saturday would have been her birthday too. It says she died in a car crash. Cleo told me she was friends with his sister. Do you think that's got something to do with it?'

'Maybe.' Dan looks up from the stairs, grateful to have something to go on. 'What was his sister's name?'

'Marnie,' I say and I hand him my phone so he can see the whole name.

There's a tense silence as Dan looks something up. He's tapping the side of his phone impatiently as he waits for a page to load.

'I found an article from the local paper . . .' He trails off as he scans the screen. 'There were two girls in the car – Marnie was driving, but the other girl survived. It says they were both drunk.'

'Does it say where?' My throat is dry as I remember Martin's face when he saw Cleo. He blames her.

'It was on the M40,' says Dan. 'It says they were driving to London. You don't think she's gone there?'

'It's got to be worth a try,' I say.

Dan gets out his phone to call the taxi, but I stop him.

'I know someone.'

Chapter 39

Luckily there's only one Dave in Oxford who's a part-time rickshaw man, part-time taxi driver, so he's not too hard to find.

'Hiya, love.' He grins, his handlebar moustache nearly at his ears. 'Fella not with you today?'

I shake my head quickly and start to explain to him about Cleo. He looks around the group and his expression becomes more serious.

'What are we looking for?'

'A mint-green Ford Fiesta,' says Arlo proudly.

'And we're about twenty minutes behind her?' Dave says and we all nod. 'Best hope the lass is a slow driver.'

I didn't even know Cleo could drive, but I don't think that would be the best thing to say. Either way I can't imagine her being a slow driver.

* * *

'Up ahead!' shouts Dan, who is sitting in the front passenger seat. 'In the lay-by.'

We all crane our necks to see. I'm wedged in between Simon and Arlo and have a very small range of movement.

There's a mint-green blob up ahead. It looks like she's overshot the lay-by though, and is on the grass verge at the side of the motorway.

Dave signals and we pull over. Dan gets out straight away and runs towards the car, and the rest of us follow.

Dan goes round the passenger side because the other side of the car is scarily close to the road. I get there a few moments later and the others hang back, so we don't crowd her. Dan's leaning half into the car and talking to Cleo. I can't see much, except that when he tries to put his arm round her she pushes him away. Dan retreats from the car and gives me a helpless look and I signal to him to let me try. He stands back, holding the door so I can get in.

I sit in the passenger seat. Cleo has her head forward on the steering wheel. Her body is shaking with sobs.

I put my hand tentatively on her back. She tenses, but doesn't stop me.

'Why did the fucking cat have to die?' she says.

'I don't know,' I say.

She leans over and puts her head on my shoulder. I put my other arm round her. We stay like that for a few minutes, while Dan hovers awkwardly in the corner of my vision.

Then Cleo sits up abruptly and sniffs. She wipes her eyes

on the back of her hands and takes a deep breath.

'Jesus.'

I think she's gradually calming down and then I notice that her expression has hardened and she is staring straight ahead without blinking. I turn towards Dan and try to signal with my eyes for him to look at her, but as I do the car vibrates and the air is filled with the sound of the engine.

Dan and I look at each other in horror and he leans back into the car.

'Cleo, don't!' he shouts.

'This is what she did,' says Cleo, her gaze still fixed straight ahead. 'I told her not to drive. I was outside the car, shouting at her, and then she started moving away and I jumped in so she wouldn't be on her own.'

She revs the engine.

'Rosie, get out,' she says.

'Cleo, please.' My voice comes out with hardly any sound.

A massive lorry speeds past us, making the whole car shake. If she'd pulled out it would have hit us.

'Cleo,' says Dan slowly. 'You need to get out of the car. Turn the engine off.'

'Make Rosie get out first,' she says and revs the engine again.

Dan pulls my arm and I slide out of the car so I'm standing next to him. My hand is still gripping the side of the seat. Relief floods through me, but I don't want to leave Cleo.

She revs the engine again and this time the car shoots forward a metre or so. Taking me with it. My arm is caught on the seat belt and I'm dragged along the grass, the door closing on me.

I dive back into the car and lunge for the handbrake. When she tries again I pull up with all my strength. The car judders violently and then stalls.

Chapter 40

The driver comes on the announcement system and starts reading out the stations.

Cleo wedges her knee up against the seat in front and looks out of the window. She hasn't said much about the girl who died – Marnie – but it's clear how she felt about her.

We were sitting on the sofa after Dave the taxi man dropped us home and I was trying to think of something else we could talk about. Something not depressing. So I blurted it out.

'You know, it's my birthday party on the weekend and I have a spare plus-one.'

Cleo considered and then nodded.

'Sure. I'll drive.'

I almost had a heart attack.

'Joke,' Cleo said. 'Too soon?'

* * *

I text Gabi to say that I need my plus-one again. She replies immediately.

```
What?! Not a boy?? Isn't that a bit soon?
I have to shuffle all the rooms round
again! P.S. CAN'T WAIT TO SEE YOU!
```

I reply telling her it's Cleo and then shove my phone in my bag because I'm nervous of the reply. I know the girls might find it really weird. Cleo used to go out with Jamie, before Mia got together with him, and the party is at Jamie's family hotel. But Cleo seemed happy to come – or indifferent. It's hard to tell with her.

She hasn't said much. She's reading her book. *On the Road*. But she's been on the same page for quite a while. I get out my Sarah Waters book.

'You know, you can talk about it if you want,' I say and find my place.

'I know,' says Cleo. She turns the page. 'I will. At some point.'

We read for a while.

'Thanks,' says Cleo.

Finally I look at my phone for Gabi's reply. She's sent a snapchat of her shouting, 'O.M.G!'

As we walk up the drive, Radleigh Castle comes into view. It is set around four huge, square towers, joined to make a square. Both of the front towers are surrounded by scaffolding. Gabi said that when the Great Hall roof fell in they decided to make repairs to the entire castle at the same time. But even as a building site the place still looms impressively.

Gabi's standing on the stone steps that lead up to the large, wooden front doors. She's wearing a smart blue dress, has her hair tied back and a serious expression on her face. I almost don't recognise her. Then when she sees me she shrieks and breaks into a mad run and she looks like Gabi again.

'ARGH! Happy birthday! And welcome!'

She leaps onto me and nearly knocks me over. When she finally releases me she looks at Cleo.

'Hey, Rosie's new plus-one.'

'Hi . . .' says Cleo.

'You have to promise you won't kill Mia in her sleep or anything. She's still terrified of you. You know, after the stealing-your-boyf drama.'

'I promise . . .' says Cleo. 'I've got Rosie to keep an eye on me.'

'Yeah,' says Gabi, sounding relieved. 'Watch out – Rosie can do a good sleeper-hold and no one knows where she learnt it.'

Gabi ushers us into the castle reception, which is through a smaller door in the right-hand turret. We have to go down a makeshift corridor through the building works and Gabi greets all the builders.

As we climb the stairs to go to our room and put our bags away, Gabi turns back to me and mouths, 'Are you okay?'

Immediately sadness floods through me and tears

spring into my eyes. But I nod and force a smile. Gabi squeezes my hand.

'You will be,' she whispers.

Walking along the corridor, with the latticed windows looking down onto the courtyard on one side and the portraits of stern-looking people in wigs on the other, Gabi starts to explain her schedule for the day and evening. She is refreshing her phone every few seconds.

'Where is Max? He's half an hour late! Worst best boy chum ever. Grrr! Canapés!'

She's looking through the window and then she rushes off to sort out whatever food-related disaster it is that she's noticed.

I'm secretly glad Max isn't here yet. It'll only make me want to ask him about Cal.

There's a squeak of floorboards behind us and we look round to see Mia. She is eyeing Cleo warily.

'All right?' she says and nods, clearly trying to act casual.

'Um, yeah,' replies Cleo. Then she starts walking away down the corridor. 'So where's our room?'

Mia goes to follow her, but pauses as she passes me.

'I'm going to clear the air.'

'Oh good luck! She's quite nice really,' I say.

'Hmm,' says Mia. 'Don't think I made the best start, saying "all right" and nodding like a man.'

I laugh and she starts to go after Cleo again, but then turns back.

'Are *you* okay?'

I nod, smile, blink a lot.

ALL GATHER AT THE FRONT OF THE CASTLE

It wasn't really necessary for Gabi to text, as we could all hear her shouting in the courtyard. Apparently there's a surprise.

I walk out onto the stone steps.

On the drive is a horse and carriage.

'We get to go twice round the block! I got it for you because you like all those films with people with bonnets in them.' Gabi beams.

'Oh my God!' I stare at her, open-mouthed. 'This is amazing, Gabi!'

She assures me that she got it 'on the cheap' – the company were here for a wedding and the driver owed her a favour because she snuck him food out of the reception.

'Now there isn't loads of room,' she tells us. 'So the actual carriage ride is just for the girls.'

We look around. It's me, Cleo, Gabi, Mia, Nish and her girlfriend, Effie.

'There aren't any boys here, Gabi,' says Nish.

'Where IS Max?' bursts out Gabi. 'He was really looking forward to meeting a horse. He says he's never seen one in real life – how mental is that? He's such a weirdo.'

Once we are sitting in the carriage we manage to get Gabi to stop calling Max and put her phone away. Twice around the block is actually a long way when the block is the grounds of Radleigh Castle. We go down a path lined with trees that has a fountain at the end and along a river, until the castle is nearly out of sight.

We come up the castle drive for the second time, the carriage bumping along on the gravel and bits of stone flying into the air, thrown by the horse's hooves.

'The castle looks awesome arriving like this,' Nish says to me.

But I don't respond.

Because standing in front of the castle in the distance are two figures. Both tall, but one lanky and the other well built, like a rugby player.

'Max!' shouts Gabi. 'God – about time. Who's that? . . . Oh.'

Everyone turns to look at me. My mouth is dry and my heart feels like it's stuck in my throat. Why is he here?

The carriage skids to a halt.

It's gone past Cal and Max, so I have my back to them now. I hear Cal greeting people and helping them get down out of the carriage, but I'm too scared to look at him. Then it's my turn. I take his hand.

For a brief second we are holding hands and my eyes meet his. Hope, excitement and fear all shoot through me at the same time and for a second Cal and I are the only two people in the world. And then it's over. The other people come back into focus and we are standing in a group outside the castle.

'So – you're here!' Gabi says to Cal.

He grins. 'I was hoping I could still be Rosie's plus-one.'

'Right!' shouts Gabi. 'Come on, Max. Help me shuffle the rooms again. Rosie – stop making friends.'

The others perform some sort of orchestrated

222

manoeuvre and all speed up at the same time, leaving me and Cal to walk into the castle together.

My heart buzzes just at the sight of him. I keep treating myself to looks as we walk.

'I hope it's okay that I came,' he says.

'Of course! Yes, no – it's brilliant!'

Stop saying things.

'I just thought – if we're going to be friends.'

It's like a kick in the chest. I try to keep my face normal as he carries on talking.

'I talked to the others this morning – I heard about Nigel. I'm gutted! I think they're having the funeral today.'

I tell him about Simon's plan to put Nigel in a burning boat and he laughs.

'They were so jealous about us coming here,' he says.

I look at him. He has a mischievous glint in his eye.

'No! We can't invite them,' I say. 'Gabi will have a breakdown.'

'Maybe I can talk her round.' He grins. 'It would be awesome, wouldn't it?'

'Yeah, it would,' I say.

There's a pause and I just look at him.

'What?' he says. He sounds like he's holding his breath.

I want to tell him how good it is to see him. How much I've missed him.

I swallow.

'Nothing.' I smile at him. One of those rubbish, awkward, fake smiles.

'Okay,' he says. And we walk inside to find Gabi.

* * *

'So when you say "a couple more people" you mean two, don't you?' says Gabi. 'Because "a couple" is two.'

'I said "a few",' says Cal, giving her a pleading look.

'You didn't,' says Gabi firmly.

We've been sitting out in the courtyard playing board games, while Gabi gets the evening party ready around us. About an hour later we hear the sound of a noisy engine approaching. Cal and I follow Gabi out to the front of the castle. A mint-green Ford Fiesta is on its way along the driveway. It skids to a halt at the end of the drive and the housemates climb out.

'Right. Who are you?' says Gabi.

There's a beat.

'We're Rosie's plus-ones,' says Arlo.

'Apparently you are,' she says. 'All *three* of you.'

Gabi starts flicking through her notepad and muttering darkly, while giving me evils. She shakes her fist at me. 'If it wasn't your birthday, Hunter!' Then she turns back to the car. 'Max is the porter and he will take your bags.'

Max appears at the top of the steps and trudges down, stopping to yank up his jeans, which always hang too low.

'Max is the porter!' says Cal. 'Where's your uniform, bro?'

'I had one for him, but he refused to wear it,' says Gabi.

Dan says that they can all take their own bags, which Max doesn't argue with, but he does give them a hand getting them out.

'Oh my God.' Dan suddenly stops as he walks towards

the steps. 'Nigel. We never had the funeral. She's still on the kitchen table!'

'Oh no, I put her in the boot,' says Arlo, who is standing next to him.

We all stare at him in stunned silence.

'There's *another* one of you?' says Gabi.

'Hey, someone's left their coat,' says Max from over by the car.

His scream echoes off the castle turrets.

Chapter 41

The next activity is swimming, but most people sit around the pool and don't go in. Jamie's in front of the doors with Mia. He looks the same as ever. Messy blond hair, stubble and a slightly bad-tempered expression with a hint of amusement. Mia has a choppy, shorter new haircut and I notice that she keeps staring off into the distance. Maybe her head is already in Australia.

Arlo sidles up to Jamie.

'Excuse me. Can we bury our cat in your grounds?' he says.

Jamie frowns and then turns to Mia. 'Who is this person?'

'His name is Arlo and he's a gatecrasher,' says Gabi, narrowing her eyes.

'So how about it? Nigel deserves a fitting send-off,' says Dan.

There's an edge of defiance to the way he grins at Jamie.

'Um, no?' says Jamie.

'Come, Jay, don't be so grumpy.' Mia waves her hand at him dismissively. 'They can bury him in the woods —'

'Her,' interrupts Dan.

'— and no one will ever know,' finishes Mia.

Jamie looks at her for a second. 'Yes, dear,' he says and then wanders off a few metres and lights a cigarette. He nearly walks into Simon, who says, 'Hey man, you got a light?'

'Yes,' says Jamie and holds out his lighter.

'Do you also have a cigarette?' says Simon.

Jamie turns back to Mia. 'Why do people I don't know keep talking to me?'

'I think we need to do some introductions,' says Gabi. She takes a deep breath.

'Right. So Jamie and Cleo used to go out and now Jamie's with Mia, who's my best friend, and I used to go out with Max, but now we're just friends – well, maybe a bit more. Anyway, why do we always have to put a label on things? So Mia used to go out with Dan, and Dan used to work here, and he keeps looking at Cleo in a funny way, so maybe something's going on there, and Rosie, who's the birthday girl – happy birthday, Rosie! – and also one of my best friends, used to go out with Cal, or maybe they're back together – I haven't heard the latest and Rosie is secretive – and Cal is Max's brother, and these people are his housemates Simon and Arlo, apparently, and our other best friend is Nish and her girlfriend is Effie and they've been together for, like, ever and they were friends with Cleo back when Cleo was going out with Jamie.'

She stops to draw breath. 'Wow, guys. As a group we should really branch out a bit more.'

Gabi is also sceptical of the cat funeral at first, until we tell her she can organise it, and then she adds it to the schedule.

'It means you get less time swimming,' she says, 'but it's your funeral . . .'

She waits.

'Oh come on, guys. That was really good!'

'I think I'll give this a miss,' says Jamie.

'Me too,' says Cleo quickly.

The other housemates and I catch each other's eyes and none of us says anything.

Mia turns back to Jamie and asks him if he's okay. He looks surprised for a moment and then his expression softens. He takes her hand and pulls her closer.

'I'm fine. Don't you worry. And don't be long at your cat funeral.'

He goes to kiss her, but then looks up and realises we are all watching. And we realise we are watching them. As one, we turn to go and leave them to have their private moment. Except Gabi, who is pulled away by Max.

A few moments later Mia catches us up. In the distance we hear Jamie as he says to Cleo, 'So, how's student life? Is it all not washing and drinking wine from mugs?'

I'm walking next to Mia. She looks back at them for just a second and then carries on.

'Do you mind them hanging out?' I ask.

'What?' she says. 'Oh no, it's not that. It's just – there's so many things to sort for Australia. Jamie's done a lot of it, but I'm still stressed. I've been a bit stroppy with him, actually – might have to get him some sort of gift to apologise for being a knob.'

She smiles at me and I return it, but my stomach twists painfully like it does every time I remember I'm not with Cal. I envy Mia and Jamie. They're so at ease with each other. It doesn't seem like they would let stupid things like jealousy wreck what they have.

Unlike me and Cal, who broke at the first sign of trouble.

The funeral is moving, if a little odd. The four housemates are the pallbearers and carry the shoebox over to a hole that Dan dug. Dan officiates and Simon reads a eulogy that Arlo has written, because Arlo hates public speaking. That bit all runs smoothly except when Simon finds Arlo's writing hard to read and instead of 'She would lick my face in the morning to wake me up' he says, 'She would kick my face every morning to wake me up.'

Cal gives a rendition of 'Everybody Wants to be a Cat'.

Nish and Effie look quite confused throughout, but are too polite to say anything. And Max stands at the back, still looking quite shaken.

When we come back Jamie and Cleo are sitting on the edge of the swimming pool, dangling their feet in the water.

Mia and I walk up behind them just as Cleo is expressing

her surprise that Jamie has been managing to hold down a job.

'But I suppose it's got to be done if you're emigrating,' she says.

'Ah, that,' says Jamie.

Mia stops dead. She stays standing there as Jamie leans towards Cleo to whisper something, just as Cleo's eyes flick over to us.

'You've buried the cat?' she says and Jamie spins round in surprise. He and Mia look at each other and the tension cuts through the air.

They are interrupted by Gabi's voice calling us all over.

'So, The Plan. Drinks and food in the courtyard, then we retire to the poolhouse to play party games. Then tomorrow a barbecue on the roof.'

'Wow, thanks Gabi,' I say.

'I wasn't told about the party games,' says Jamie. 'Just so everyone knows.'

Nish is also looking sceptical. 'Shouldn't we be playing poker or something? Now that we're all adults.'

'Exactly!' says Gabi. 'We are all adults. And we're all about to go off and do adulty things, like going to uni or getting jobs or abandoning our best friends to live in Australia. So we should play games now, before we're too busy giving birth or shopping for curtains.'

'What are the games?'

'Truth or dare, karaoke and pin the willy on the man,' says Gabi.

Chapter 42

'I'm going to need a stiff gin before I pin the willy on the man,' says Nish.

I'm about to speak, but Mia cuts in.

'Don't worry, Gabi made an alternative version just for you,' she says. 'Pin the fanny on the woman.'

Nish looks horrified. 'No!'

''Fraid so – Effie is playing it now.'

From the other side of the room we hear Effie's loud laugh. She has a blindfold on and Gabi is spinning her round. Two life-size cartoon pictures of a man and a woman, drawn on large sheets of paper, are stuck to the wall.

'Who drew them?' I say and Mia raises her hand.

'Gabi cornered me in my room last week with paper and a Sharpie. The only bit where I was really worried was when she told me I was going to be drawing round Max. But it turned out that was just the outline of the body.'

We all burst out laughing and then I notice that Nish is still watching Effie.

'Is everything okay with you two?'

'Fine! Fine. Yeah, fine.' Nish shrugs.

'So you're still pretending that you're not worried about her going to Paris?' says Mia, her eyebrow raised.

'Yep,' says Nish with a tight smile. 'There's no point. If she's going to leave me, she's going to leave, whether or not I go mental about it.'

Well, I suppose going mental didn't get me anywhere.

Over at the karaoke Max and Cal are duetting, with Max as Jay-Z and Cal as Beyoncé. I watch Cal and think about the meal, when the housemates gave me their gift. I'd completely forgotten about it, but then there hadn't been a day when we were all in the house together this week except for the cat day.

They gave me a signed Quentin Blake print. A scene from *Matilda*, which was my favourite book as a child. And they could only have known that from Cal. It's sitting at the side of the pool house in a plastic bag and I get a rush of warmth whenever I look at it. The only pang of disappointment I got was that in the card Cal just signed his name. He usually draws a funny cartoon.

'Hey,' says Cal.

He's appeared behind me as I was looking at the card.

'Hey,' I say, trying not to show that everything in me surges when I see him.

'I wanted to say something – and it's a bit easier to say after a beer.'

I don't let myself get excited this time.

'Sure – what?'

'The stuff you found on my computer – it's just silly. The kind of stuff the guys send round to each other. I mean, I can't pretend I didn't – you know – enjoy it, but it didn't have anything to do with the way I thought about you.'

He looks around while he's talking and ruffles his hair. Then we look at each other and laugh.

'Argh,' he says. 'Why is this awkward? This is you. I'm not awkward around you. I guess I just want you to know it wasn't because I was missing anything. You were more than enough for me.'

I smile at him then.

'So you don't wish I was a spanking lesbian?'

He does a face like he's considering it and I hit him on the arm.

'No,' he says. 'You're perfect as you.'

We look at each other and it's too much. I look down. Then I think of something I can say.

'I've decided to drop out from my course.'

His eyebrows rise in surprise. 'Hey, just because the other cool kids are doing it . . .'

'I'm going to do primary school teaching,' I say. 'Next September. And this year I'll be a classroom assistant.'

'Where will you do that?'

I stop. It was going to be Oxford when I planned it.

'I don't know yet – home, probably.'

'That's awesome,' says Cal. 'You'll be great. You got my cousins reading books rather than destroying the house. My aunt would probably employ you herself.'

'Thanks, Cal. I'm really looking forward to it, actually. I mean not that there's anything wrong with business – I'm sure Nish is going to be a terrifyingly successful businesswoman. I just don't think it's for me.'

'It's really cool.' His smile spreads over his face. He looks genuinely happy for me.

'How are things with you?' I say.

'Ah well, I got a new job!'

He tells me he's going to be a crewmember at the Boathouse and take people on boating tours. Apparently he got talking to them when he was down there and they think he'd be just right for it.

'Something where you talk to people all day – I think you've found your perfect job.' I smile at him.

'Ha – yeah!' He nods. 'And I've found a local rugby club to try out for, so I can keep that up while I work out the next step.'

'It's not easy, is it?' I say.

'No!' he agrees. It feels like we are standing a bit closer with every sentence. 'It seems much easier to work out what's wrong for you, than what's right,' he carries on.

'But in a way it's quite exciting,' I say. 'You could do anything!'

He looks at me in surprise. 'You think I could do anything?'

I hold his gaze. 'Of course I do.'

'Truth or dare!' calls Gabi. 'Everyone round the coffee table.'

Cal and I wander over to the table where the others are slowly gathering. Everyone looks a bit apprehensive. Effie comes over and joins Nish and Mia on the sofa. She puts her arm round Nish's neck and gives Nish a big kiss on the cheek and Nish pushes her away with a frown because she doesn't like public displays of affection. But then I see she puts her hand over Effie's.

Jamie is sitting on a bar stool next to the kitchen counter and refusing to join in. But he's the only one. Even Cleo comes over and sits down after Dan persuades her. Cal is a few people along from me. Out of the corner of my eye I can see his hand with his Leeds Festival wristband. This whole year I've been telling him it's really grim he's still got it on, but now even that is one of the details about him that makes my heart ache.

Gabi has a proper spinner in the middle and cards prepared in two piles. The first person it lands on is Arlo. He picks 'dare' in what must be a rare fit of confidence and then he immediately regrets it because his dare is to jump in the pool.

'But I've got nice trousers on!'

Poor Arlo is given a helping hand by Cal and Simon and soon he is back in the circle, soaked and shivering. Then Dan chooses 'dare' and has to eat a teabag. Mia shouts out that he's already done that because they used to do eating challenges when they worked at Radleigh together. Jamie puts his glass down on the counter loudly and Mia's eyes flick over to him, but she doesn't respond. I'm beginning to think I jinxed them when I was thinking how amazing they were earlier. Simon asks for truth and is asked to name his secret crush. He looks over at Nish and Effie and says he's always thought he would be able to convert lesbians. Nish gives him a stony glare and Effie bursts out laughing.

Then Max also picks truth and his card says, *Tell someone what you really think of them.*

Max looks at Gabi.

His usually thoughtful face looks even more serious and his eyebrows are raised. He swallows.

Then Max looks over at Cal. 'You should change your shorts more often.'

There's a ripple of laughter and Gabi quickly leans over to spin again, not meeting Max's eye.

It lands on me. There are noises of surprise when I pick 'dare'. But I'm not really up for revealing secrets.

I see Gabi fiddling with the cards and then she hands me one face down.

'Don't I get to pick?' I say.

Gabi shakes her head.

I turn the card over. It says, *Kiss Cal.* I give Gabi a look and then everyone else starts asking what's on the card. Nish grabs it off me and reads it out.

When I look up I see Cal is already looking at me. He half smiles at me.

'Well, you've go to do what the card says.'

I lean behind the others sitting on the sofa and so does he.

I sit back down and nearly fall over. I'm dizzy and my heart is pounding in my chest. It feels like my whole body is tingling.

I'm barely concentrating on the game and suddenly realise that everyone is calling to Jamie.

'Not playing,' he says. 'Leave me alone!'

'It's pointing right at you!' says Mia.

'Thanks for the loyalty, dear,' says Jamie drily.

'Truth or dare?' says Gabi.

'Truth. Dare. Whatever – I don't care,' he says.

'Truth!' says Gabi and picks up the cards.

'Have you saved the money for Australia?' says Mia.

Jamie looks at her. No one speaks.

'Do you really want to do this here?' he says.

'Have you?' says Mia.

Jamie's eyebrows knit into a frown and he breathes in. Then he looks at Mia again. His usual confidence is gone and he looks scared.

'No.'

Mia stands up and walks out of the open French windows. Jamie goes after her.

'That's what happens when you don't play by the rules,' mutters Gabi, shuffling the cards.

We all look around the circle and seem to make an unspoken group decision that the game is over.

Cal is the one to break the silence.

'I think Rosie wants to go swimming again.'

I look up. 'What?'

Cal leaps over from his side of the sofa and scoops me up. I wriggle and protest as he carries me out of the doors and everyone else follows. I scream as he throws me in. It's a heated pool, but being submerged in tepid water is still a bit of a shock. There's a huge splash as Gabi pushes Cal in and then another one as she pushes Max. Soon everyone is either pushed or jumps in voluntarily and a massive water fight begins.

I swim towards Cal and splash him and in response he picks me up again and throws me into the air. I'm getting a weird sense of déjà vu as I go for him again. Maybe we are gradually getting back into sync.

Chapter 43

'It was a stubbly person!'

Cleo rolls over and peers drowsily at me. 'What?'

'It was a stubbly person with hairy arms!'

'What are you talking about?'

'The person who carried me the night I fainted. I didn't remember before, but Cal picking me up by the swimming pool brought it all back!'

Cleo sits up in bed. We're in the master bedroom, which had been reserved for me and Cal, but after all the room shuffling Cal is sharing a room with Dan.

The four-poster bed is so big that they could probably fit in here as well. Although obviously that would be a bit odd.

'Okay, yes,' says Cleo. 'Cal carried you. But he said not to tell you if you didn't remember.'

'Why?'

'He said he's not the guy for you. But he wants you to be happy. That's why he was staying away. When he did try to get you back and it was such a disaster, he realised he'd had it right the first time.'

I swallow and my heart thumps weirdly in my chest.

'And did he see me kissing that guy in the window?'

Cleo bites her lip and nods. 'Yeah.'

I roll over and face away from her. I don't say anything else. I think she thinks I'm asleep. But I'm awake for the rest of the night.

About an hour after we talked, I hear her leave the room.

Chapter 44

'Whoa, it all lurches when you lean over the edge, doesn't it?' says Effie as we stand by the wall at the front of the castle roof. The grounds and the hills in the distance are bathed in sunshine.

'Don't lean over then,' snaps Nish.

'Chillax,' says Effie. 'I thought you were getting me a burger.'

Nish rolls her eyes and walks off towards the barbecue.

'Thanks, lover!' laughs Effie.

'She's being like that because she's worried,' I say.

'I know, silly woman,' says Effie. 'I have a plan, though. I've hidden a ticket to Paris in her bag, for the first weekend I'm there. She hasn't found it yet. I thought it might help show her that she'll be a part of my life there too – from the beginning. What do you reckon?'

I smile. 'She'll love it. Well, she'll pretend not to, but she will.'

We are quiet for a while, just enjoying the feeling of the sun on our arms and listening to the sound of people chatting and the sizzling of the barbecue. There's the occasional shriek from Gabi as she runs around organising things. She's in a bright pink dress, so impossible to miss in every way.

The only person who is missing is Jamie. Mia says she hasn't seen him all day.

And Cleo didn't appear until about midday. I haven't had the chance to ask her where she went.

'What about you and your man?' says Effie. 'Things on the mend there?'

I look at Cal. He's laughing loudly at something Dan has said. On his plate is the most obscenely big burger I've ever seen.

'I don't know.'

After a few hours we decide to go inside for a bit to get out of the sun. There's this lounge-type room upstairs called the Window Room – because, unsurprisingly, it has a lot of windows – so we gather in there. Cal sits behind me and gradually I move back so I'm leaning against his arm.

Mia has hardly said anything all day. Then suddenly she slams down her glass of Coke.

'I can't believe he's ruined my trip. We were supposed to see in the New Year in Australia. Christmas was going to be a barbecue on the beach.'

The other conversations around the room trail off and everyone's attention turns to Mia. Her eyes are blazing.

'You know what? I'm going to go anyway.'

She stands up determinedly and starts walking across the room. There's a flash of bright pink and before we know it Gabi is up and has rugby tackled Mia to the ground.

'You're not going.'

Mia tries to climb to her feet, with Gabi still clinging to her. 'I didn't mean I was going *right now*! I'm going to get my phone and bring the flights forward.'

She breaks free and runs into the corridor, but Gabi is close behind. She grabs Mia round the middle and lifts her up, while Mia's legs kick around in the air.

'Get OFF me!' she cries.

'NO!' says Gabi firmly and the struggle continues.

We've all gathered at the door. No one is quite sure what to do.

'She's pretty strong!' says Cal.

'Oh she is.' Max nods wisely.

The struggle continues down the corridor, until they reach a door, which I think is a bathroom for staff to use. Gabi has her arms round Mia's waist. She lifts her up off the ground again and practically throws her through the toilet door.

She grabs the doorknob and slams the door shut. Mia's cries of protest from the other side are muffled.

'Now,' says Gabi, keeping a firm grip on the door handle, 'I've done this so that I can say something and you'll listen. You can't just run off without finding out why

Jamie's done this. All you think about is the next place you're going. And all you talk about is how crap it is round here and how you want to get out. Maybe Jamie just wants to hang out with you and do something normal, like watch TV or go shopping or get your nails done, instead of planning the next trip.'

Gabi's voice chokes a bit at the end. She frowns and grips the doorknob harder. Mia says something and Gabi puts her ear to the door to listen.

'Yes maybe it's not Jamie who wants to get his nails done with you,' Gabi replies.

Mia says something else.

'I know you do. It's just you're always going off. So sometimes it doesn't feel like it,' says Gabi, more quietly, and then she puts her ear to the door again.

'Yeah it probably is a better idea to talk in the same room.'

She lets go to allow Mia to come out. The doorknob turns but the door doesn't open. It turns again and then back the other way and still nothing happens. Gabi tries opening it and the same thing happens.

'I think it's jammed!' she says. We all look around to see who would be the best person to break down a door. That's when I notice that Cleo has gone.

Dear Marnie,

One more letter. And then I will let you go. I need to start making friends who are a bit less dead.

But someone needs to hear the end of the story. At the moment you are still the only person I can tell everything to. I think that will change – I think there are people I can start talking to now. But it takes time. And I can't tell it to the cat.

His room was the one at the end of the corridor, next to the window.

'Couldn't keep away?' he said when he opened the door.

I told him I slept-walked and took a wrong turn. And he stepped outside and pulled the door shut, so as not to wake a sleeping (snoring) Cal.

We stood opposite each other. The shadows cast shapes on his face so I couldn't see him properly.

I asked him if it reminded him of the night the lights went out.

'Yeah,' he said, 'and we never really talked about that.'

We both took a step closer.

'Dan?' I said. I could hear both our hearts beating, but I couldn't tell whose was whose.

He said, 'Yes, Cleo?'

And I said it. Those three little words. 'Let's be friends?'

He reached for my hand. 'I thought you'd never ask.'

I couldn't look at him while I spoke, so I looked down at his hand and said, 'I know you hate it that girls always say you're lovely and funny and they want to be friends with you, but I've never had a best friend. And it turns out you are lovely and funny. So I could do a lot worse.'

He nodded and said, 'I know,' in a mock-arrogant tone.

I told him it would be ages before I could even think about being more than friends with anyone. And he said 'I know' again and he pulled me towards him.

I asked him what he was doing and he replied that he was giving me a hug so I'll stop babbling. I let him hug me and I rested my head on his shoulder. For a while we just stood like that and I felt his chest go up and down.

'Perhaps there are upsides to losing out to the bad boy,' Dan said.

I turned my head towards him. 'There never was a bad boy.'

Next on the list, Mia and Jamie.

I'd had the urge to bang their heads together and tell them to sort it out since Mia came and talked to me.

All this time I thought she never got what she did wrong when she stole Jamie. I thought an apology would be empty, because if she had the chance she'd do it all again. But she did understand. I'd thought for one stupid moment over that summer that she and I could be friends, before she went off with him. And she knew that. She said she dealt with it by telling herself I was a bitch.

When she started going on about going to Australia on her own I knew it was time to act. I knew where he'd be. I'm not totally sure I was supposed to go up the turret with all the scaffolding there, but the builders had gone home and I thought if he could manage it so could I.

The wooden Wendy house was the only thing not covered in plastic sheeting. It's the place that Jamie and his sister always used to come to get away from their douchebag dad. Jamie must have told the builders not to touch it, which is typical him.

I put my head round the door and there he was. Sitting against the wall with his chin resting on his fist. I told him for God's sake enough with the brooding. Bad boys aren't hot any more.

He looked up and laughed. Then he patted the cushion next to him.

Then he said as I sat down that he had well and truly screwed this up.

'Don't be so dramatic,' I said. 'Just tell her the truth.'

He took a while to convince and kept saying how he'd been lying to her for weeks and surely he couldn't come back from that. I said he should try. That it was better than giving up. I really should consider life coaching. First Rosie with her career, now Jamie with his love life. Except life coaches probably aren't supposed to say, 'Stop being a whiny little bitch.'

Which I said to Jamie, rather than Rosie, obviously.

Finally I dragged him out of the Wendy house and onto the turret. The day was becoming a warm summer evening and the sun was glinting through the trees.

Jamie changed the subject and told me he couldn't believe I was 'dating the pot washer'. I told him Dan and I are just friends. He said he thought I didn't do friends, so I shot back that I didn't think he did falling in love. He nodded and said, 'Touché.'

Then he lit a cigarette and held one out to me. I shook my head and told him I promised Dan I'd quit.

'Bloody hell,' he said and took a drag.

'Oh, fuck it. I'll have one last one. No one will know.' Jamie laughed and handed me the box.

As we came down the tower stairs Jamie asked me where Mia was and I told him she was probably still in the bathroom. Jamie looked at me and asked why.

I said, 'Gabi shut her in. She was being difficult. Then the lock jammed.'

Jamie looked impressed and said he would remember that. 'If she takes me back.' Then he dusted his hands together and strode off into the courtyard. In completely the opposite direction to the door that led inside.

I called after him as he reached the wall. Then I realised what he was doing and I yelled that I wasn't sure it was a particularly good idea.

That part of the wall was clear of scaffolding, so he started clambering, very unsteadily, up a wooden trellis that led up to the bathroom window. As he reached up to the windowsill one of his feet slipped and he yelled out, 'Bugger!'

Mia, obviously hearing the commotion, appeared at the window and was looking around with a confused expression.

I waved at her and she looked even more confused, which was fair enough.

I pointed to the wall in front of the window and tried to mouth 'Jamie' as clearly as possible. But Mia

248

peered out of the window and shook her head.

I shouted, 'Ja–mie!' and pointed at the wall.

But Mia shook her head and I could see her saying, 'I can't hear you.' And then I saw her hand move upwards and I realised she was about to open the window, just as Jamie had put both of his hands on the windowsill.

I waved my arms frantically and called out to her to stop, but it was too late. The two halves of the window swung out. One of Jamie's hands was knocked off the sill and his feet flailed around as he tried to get a grip on the trellis again. Somehow he'd managed to keep his other hand on the sill. It was the only thing keeping him up there.

Mia leaned out and yelled, 'Jamie?'

'Hello, darling!' said Jamie.

Once I could see that most of Jamie was inside the window I left them to it while I went to find the others, who were still outside the bathroom door. I explained the real story.

Jamie's on an internship for a literary agency. Or as he put it, 'Turns out I'm good at reading.' It happened when he got talking to a customer at the restaurant he was working in. But the job pays next to nothing, so he knew that by taking it he wouldn't be able to save for the trip. He kept trying to tell Mia but chickening out, and just hoped that something would happen to sort it out, 'like one of my rich uncles dying'.

Then the agent suggested he apply to uni through clearing. He phoned up and got in. He's due to start an

English degree in September.

As I finished telling them, there was a sudden crash and the door swung open, juddering with the shock, and Jamie and Mia fell into the hallway in a heap.

Mia mumbled that she'd 'put her foot in the bin', while blushing bright red, scrambling to her feet and smoothing down her skirt.

Jamie sat up and said, 'I have that effect on women.'

So Mia's still going to Australia and Jamie's going to uni, but they're going to try the long distance thing. You could see them clinging to each other that little bit more. Making the most of now. Well, the next few months, as Mia is delaying leaving until after Gabi's birthday.

I hope it works out for them. Really. If you've got it, you should cling on to it with all you've got, because you never know when it could be gone.

I'm disgustingly soppy these days, didn't anyone tell you?

Then there's Rosie and Cal. I don't know what I can do there. But if either of them has any sense, they'll realise how in love they are.

Thank you for showing me what it's like.

I don't know how to end this. I don't want to say goodbye to you. I never did.

Love you always.
Cleo x

Chapter 45

'Where is the champagne?' Gabi demands. 'Jamie and Mia went to get it ages ago. They better not be drinking it all. Or "doing it"!'

'Chill, baby,' says Max and she stops. Almost instinctively I meet Cal's eye and we share a look that says 'Wow, things have changed.' I draw out the excuse to look at him.

And then Jamie and Mia return and Max takes a champagne bottle from the ice bucket. He starts trying to pour it out, spills some and Gabi grabs it off him, calling him a 'lumbering ape' and the universe returns to normal.

Mia taps her nail against the glass. 'Toast! Everyone grab your booze. So I just wanted to say, happy birthday, Rosie!' Everyone echoes this and lifts their glasses. 'And I know Rosie hates speeches, but she wanted Gabi to know that this is all perfect – thanks so much, Gabz.'

Gabi, who is standing next to me, grabs me and gives me a big kiss on the cheek.

'Also, this weekend has been awesome,' Mia continues. 'Well, apart from Jamie nearly dying. And Gabi locking me in a toilet.'

Gabi nods proudly. 'Won't try running away again, will you?'

Mia grins at her and then shares a look with Jamie. One of those looks where you are completely in sync with each other. Like Cal and I used to have. Like we could have again?

'So I think we should promise to do this every year. All of us. Even the uninvited plus-ones.' Mia gives me a smile.

'Hear, hear!' says Jamie.

Everyone goes to drink, but we are interrupted by a shout from Gabi.

'Wait! I want to do one, too.'

She totters to the front of the group in her massive heels. Then she clears her throat. 'Oh, what's this?' Gabi opens her bag and pulls out a card. 'Why, it's another truth or dare card! Who wants to read it? Max?'

Max looks startled and confused. 'Um, okay.' He takes it from her. 'It says, *Gabi, what are you doing next year?*'

Heads turn back to Gabi. From the expressions on everyone's faces it is clear that she's the only one who has any idea what's going on.

'That's an interesting question. Thank you, Max. Well, the thing is . . .' Gabi takes a deep breath in. Her eyebrows knit together in a worried frown and she's fidgeting with her fingers. I think she is actually *nervous*. 'Max, I've arranged to move to Leeds and I didn't tell you!'

Max stares at her. And then he goes to speak.

But Gabi interrupts him. 'I'm doing TV Production at Leeds Met and I move next week.'

Max goes to speak again.

'I'm living down the road from you!' she blurts quickly before he can start talking.

Max's eyes are wide. We watch him, trying to process the last few minutes and wondering how he's going to react.

'Cool,' he says.

Gabi's eyes are wide. 'Is it?'

'Course!' Max shrugs. 'Why wouldn't it be?'

'Because, you know. We're sort of half-couple, half-friends and everyone thinks we're weird.'

'I don't know what we are.' Max smiles. 'But whatever it is, I like it.'

'Oh, okay,' Gabi says. 'Because I thought it would be really cool – I'll be learning all about how to make TV programmes and there's a really good TV society and I thought you could do the music for the programmes I make.' She's talking at a million miles an hour and her face keeps breaking out into a smile.

'I'd like that,' says Max.

The group dissolves into chatting again. Except when I look over at Cal I see that he isn't talking. He was watching Max and Gabi for a while. Then he looked down at the floor.

Things start flashing through my brain. Cal taking my hand and getting me to stand up in the rickshaw. Telling me he loved me when I was under all that exam stress and needed to hear it. Telling me again in front of everyone at the members' club without caring what they thought. And the way he looked like he didn't believe me when I said he could do anything.

'Wait!'

Everyone looks around to see who's shouted this time.

It's me.

I look at Cal, who is watching me with a surprised expression. But when our eyes meet he does that smile where it looks like he's trying not to smile too much.

My heart is thumping, but I hold his gaze.

'I've got something to say as well.'

Chapter 46

I hear a shuffling behind me. I turn round to see Leon, frowning and fiddling with the frayed sleeve of his school jumper.

'I finished *Matilda*,' he says. 'It was, like . . . good.

'That's great, Leon,' I say. 'It was my favourite when I was your age, too.'

He nods and fiddles with his sleeve again.

'You know I'm going to be with Year Six next term?' I say as I'm putting on my coat and scarf. 'You'll have to put up with me every day instead of once a week.'

He looks up sharply. 'Are you still doing my reading lessons?'

I nod. 'Yeah! I've got some really good ones lined up. And *The Witches* for you to take home over Christmas if you want.'

He shrugs. 'Okay.'

Then he gets a crumpled envelope out of his pocket.

'My mum made me do you a card. Bye.' He puts the card on the table and then turns and runs out of the door.

I open it. On the front is a penguin in a Christmas hat and inside he's drawn me and him at a table with an open book in front of us. On the book pages it says, *Thanks for your help with my reading*. Behind us is a bookshelf where he's written the titles of the books we've been reading. There's *Wimpy Kid* and *Matilda* and *The Subtle Knife*, which we haven't read, but I told him it was my favourite.

He's drawn some other cartoons too – a 'super death shark' and Santa holding a gun. I put the card in my bag because it's made me feel emotional and I don't want any of the teachers to see me cry. Again. Last week it was the Year Five play and before that it was Celia's creative writing work about 'The Pig Who Lost His Mum'. Apparently by the time I'm teaching on the course I'll be immune to it all, but not just yet.

I ding the bell for the Queen's Lane stop and stand up. The bus lurches to a halt. I run over the road in a gap in the traffic and head towards the archway into the garden. We haven't been able to come here in the last few weeks because it shuts early in winter, but school finished at one today. I reach the second garden and he's there – on Will and Lyra's bench.

'Did you cry again today?' he says as I sit down.

'Yeah,' I say. 'Leon gave me a Christmas card.'

I take it out and show him and he admires Leon's artistic

skills (although we both agree that I should tell Mrs Roberts about the gun-toting Santa).

Then I notice a hamper next to the bench.

'I thought you might have time for a chilly picnic before house Christmas drinks,' he says.

'I've always got time for a chilly picnic,' I say.

'Do I need to bring anything to the house?' he asks as we start to unpack the hamper, which is tricky with gloves on. 'I've made my spectacular mince pies.'

'That will be fine – you don't have to worry about impressing them any more. They love you!'

It's hilarious how nervous Cal was when he first met my housemates. I guess it's because he knows how important they can be.

'I thought of another thing I could do today,' says Cal.

'Oh yeah?' I say, looking through the food selection. He's made me a salmon bagel. Cal texts me jokey ideas for his future career most days. This week it was Mud Wrestler, Butler in the Buff and Space Cowboy.

'Sports agent,' he says.

I look up. That's a real one.

'Well, I'm going to look into it anyway.'

He starts looking for something in the hamper and doesn't meet my eye so I just tell him to let me know if he needs any help with looking up stuff and he says that would be cool.

I pick up a can of Coke and try to open it, which again is tricky while wearing gloves. Cal opens his and we tap them together.

'Cheers!' we both say and then laugh.

'Can you make another speech?' he says, grinning.

'No – you're never getting one out of me again,' I say. 'One heartfelt, rambling, slightly snotty speech should be enough.'

'The snot was the best bit,' says Cal. 'But I do agree with Mia that you shouldn't have opened with the bit about kissing the guy called Paedo.'

I'm about to reach into the hamper for the salmon bagel when I feel his arm around me. I lean my head on him and we sit there. And, for once, I don't think I have anything to worry about.

My Top 5 Acknowledgements

1. Everyone at Piccadilly Press, because you are awesome and you always think of the readers you know so well. Brenda, because this all began with you. Melissa, because you always understand what I'm on about and send me miming videos. Shane, because your editorial comments made me rethink a lot of things (except the one about absinthe being nice – it is rank).

2. Anne Clark, because you are the best agent in the world.

3. Catnip people, past and present (listen up, Non, Pip and Robert). Because all the things you've taught me about children's books and publishing have blown my tiny mind. And you don't complain when I have been up late writing and I turn up to work looking a bit like I've died.

4. Suzy, because you are my fabby pally and will be in all

the books. Hazel (yeaaaaahh), Edd, Ruth, the Man, the Bone, Laura, Lorna, Lizzie, Claire, Tanye, Haslet, Tess, Anna, Celia and Ryan. Because these books are really about having best friends.

5. Bloggers (listen up, Jim). Because, despite being horrendously busy, you take the time to write things that can make someone deliriously happy and remember why they love books.

And another. Because I do like to ramble on.

6. Tom. Because you are the best thing.

Have you read ...

Irresistible

LIZ BANKES

Mia's new summer job at a posh country club
is hard work, but fun, especially when a romance
develops with hunky Dan.

But Mia is drawn to Jamie too – sexy, rich and bored,
he's got everything he could ever want, but gets
his kicks messing with people's lives.

Even though Mia knows that getting involved with
Jamie is a bad idea, there's something so dangerously
exciting about him, she just can't resist.

Undeniable

From the author of Irresistible

LIZ BANKES

Don't miss . . .

Undeniable

LIZ BANKES

Gabi is so excited – she's spending the summer
working as a runner on her favourite TV show.
It's a dream come true! Plus it's perfect for
distracting her from The Break-Up –
especially with all those gorgeous actors around.

And then there's Spencer: student, extra, expert flirt.
Everything with him is fun, exciting – and uncertain.
Things between them are hotting up when he lands
a minor role on the show. So is it make or break for
them? Is Spencer undeniably the one for Gabi?

piccadillypress.co.uk/teen

Go online to discover:

☆ more books you'll love

☆ competitions

☆ sneak peeks inside books

☆ fun activities and downloads

Find us on Facebook for exclusive competitions, giveaways and more!
www.facebook.com/piccadillypressbooks

☆ Follow us on Twitter
@PiccadillyPress